NO
STRINGS

NO STRINGS

MILA HART

Edited by
WALLFLOWER EDITS

Cover by
VANILLA LILY DESIGNS

Through thick and thin...

"Carter! What the hell are you doing?" Nick screamed as I ran into the burning building, pulling my helmet over my head as I went.

Nick was as tenured as I was, but the rest of the men on the ground, except for the captain, weren't. While they dicked around trying to formulate a plan and two more engines pulled up, I took a risk that I knew better than to take. Firefighters should never go into a building alone. But when a life hung in the balance, the rules went out the window. I had no idea what would be on the other side of that door, but waiting for a ladder to the fifth floor wasn't an option.

The doorman ran alongside me, opened the entrance when we reached it, and pointed me toward the stairs. The visibility on the ground level was fine, and smoke hadn't entered the inside of the stairwell, either. I took each flight as quickly as I could. Four sets of stairs with seventy-five pounds of gear was only possible at break-neck speed when adrenaline coursed through me. I prayed to God there was only one person involved. I'd never get out more than that on my own, and Lord help me if there were an adult and a child.

Heavy footfalls of another man echoed behind me, but I didn't turn or wait to see who it was. I breathed heavily through the mask as I found my way to the penthouse. Smoke billowed under the door, tickling the carpet with embers. Each crackle sparked confetti flames that danced at my feet.

"Fire department!" I could feel the heat from the other side, and I wondered if the entire apartment was engulfed; hopefully, whoever was inside had found a pocket of air or opened a window.

The knob didn't budge when I tried to turn it, no one answered when I called out again, and right as Nick sidled up next to me, I slammed my Halligan tool into the frame and kicked down the door. Glass blew out from somewhere inside, and I was lucky I hadn't been caught in a backdraft.

A sea of fire rolled in through the entrance I'd just busted through, and the waves came in like a tsunami. There was no telling what had started the blaze, but there wouldn't be anything left by the time we got it put out.

Thick, black smoke hung in the air, and flares slid up the walls surrounding us. "Hello?" The living room appeared to be empty, but as I moved farther back with Nick at my heels, more men came at our rear, fanning out to check the perimeter.

Water started to pour in through the broken windows, and smoke chased freedom into the night air. The only light in the penthouse came from the inferno surrounding me. Sweat trickled down my neck and back, and the heat became oppressive. I refused to give up until I found the person I'd seen in the window. With each step I took, the fire followed me deeper into the apartment.

I'd nearly reached the end of the hall and

had come up empty-handed. There was no way out. Whoever I'd seen was still in here, hiding, and it was unlikely they could hear me call out over the roar of the sirens and the fire. The oxygen pumped into my mask, and the hollow echo of my breathing made it difficult for me to differentiate the sounds. But flames and smoke weren't unique, they had patterns and moved the same way regardless of where they burned. One thing they never did was sit still.

Even without much visibility, there was no doubt the lump near the window was a human being. And if my memory served me, it was the same window I'd seen a figure in. In seconds, I'd scooped her into my arms. Her long hair covered her face and arms, and somehow, her robe had stayed wrapped around her when I'd lifted her from the floor.

There wasn't time for any type of medical intervention, and the best I'd be able to do was get her oxygen once I'd gotten on the other side of this blaze. Nick was still at my back, but he turned to lead us out as soon as I had her secure in my embrace.

"Come on lady, don't die on me." I talked to

myself as much as I did to her. I didn't know if she could hear me or not. All I knew was if it were me, I'd want to know someone was with me. "Hang in there." *Fuck.*

Chapter One

Nights like these were highly anticipated. I got to let loose—more so than normal—and spend time with my friends. None of us were interested in men who wanted relationships, so we had a handful of local joints that catered to the needs of ladies like us. Clubs were our first choice—typically those owned by my daddy. That's where the men who didn't use dating apps hung out, and I knew what I was getting. I could mingle, observe, and then decide whether or not I had any interest in spending time one on one.

I checked myself in the mirror to ensure my new amethyst dress wasn't as short as it felt. The cold air of my penthouse hit my exposed thighs when I squatted to see how far it rode up as I moved. Satisfied with the appraisal, I rummaged through my closet until I found the perfect pair of silver, strappy heels. They weren't exactly comfortable, but they were super cute, and with a drink or two, I wouldn't really feel them anyway.

"You look amazing." Riley—my best friend and partner in crime—met me in my living room dressed to kill.

"You too." I smiled and posed for the picture when she held up her phone. The flash nearly blinded me in the soft light of my apartment, and I almost fell on top of her when I sat on the couch. "Gabby's on her way."

There was a third person that rounded out our trifecta, although Gabby didn't get to go out much. As a nurse, she typically worked the night shift, and her schedule rarely lined up with ours. But the stars had aligned, and tonight we were carpooling, with Gabby as the designated driver. While none of us were big drinkers, we were socially responsible.

"Good. I'm starving." Riley put her hand on her flat stomach. "I barely ate a thing to make sure I fit into this dress. Why can't we just go out in sweats? It would be a hell of a lot more comfortable than tight clothes and makeup, and men would know what they're really getting." Riley giggled and tugged at her blond curls, pulling them up into a ponytail, exposing her long neck and strong shoulders.

She had this modelesque stature that she never used to her advantage. Riley could have graced runways all around the globe, but she'd opted to work in advertising instead of living off her looks. Personally, I thought her career choice in marketing was boring, but she loved doing it, so after the first couple of years of fighting with her, I'd given up.

"You should have eaten, so the alcohol doesn't take over. I did." I shrugged. I hadn't had a ton to eat, but I knew better than to go out for a night on the town with nothing in my stomach. That had resulted in far more bad decisions than I cared to admit.

She narrowed her eyes and glared at me through the tiny slits, and I couldn't stop myself from laughing. "Yeah, well, you can get away with stuff like that. You have an ass; I, however, do not. If I wear fitted clothes, I'll look like an upside-down ant after a meal."

The visual had me giggling despite the death stare I received from my friend. Thankfully, Gabby interrupted the moment with a group text to let us know she was parked out front—like she didn't know Riley and I were in the same room.

We left my penthouse apartment and met Gabby on the ground floor. She had the top down on her Audi, knowing it would draw attention. What she didn't realize was that it wasn't the car the boys stared at; it was her skinny jeans and crop top. That was as dressed up as she got, and it was all she ever needed. Men swooned when she walked into a room, and she was oblivious to it all.

"Hey, girls!" Gabby squealed through a brilliant smile.

I held the seat forward while Riley managed to get into the back where she'd have room to stretch out her long-ass legs, and then I climbed into the front.

"You two always look fantastic." Gabby glanced down at her own outfit. "I should have dressed up more...." Except she never did. She pulled out of the parking lot and into the street as I waved off her excuse for going casual.

I situated myself in the leather seat, trying to accommodate the restrictions my dress—it might as well have been a corset—placed on my body. If I could get away with jeans and a shirt, I would absolutely do it. But I had to work a little harder than Gabby and Riley. I had an image to maintain and a reputation to uphold. Being a socialite came with certain responsibilities, things Gabby and Riley took for granted because they were my friends—not that I begrudged them that right.

Gabby grinned and turned up the music, most of which was lost in the rush of the wind and the noise of Friday-night traffic. She was probably the most carefree of the three of us and definitely the smartest. Her dark hair and olive skin brought out her Italian ancestry, but it didn't matter how many hot guys hit on her. She'd met Mr. Right while the rest of us were playing with Mr. Right Now and currently sported a rather noticeable diamond on her left hand. They were waiting until he finished his residency to actually tie the knot, but it had been quite the scandal when the relationship had started at the hospital.

Riley and I, on the other hand, lived very

single and "free" lives. I didn't buy into the idea that women couldn't have as much fun as men; they just needed to do so with a little less fanfare, so the press didn't catch wind—the paparazzi could be a bitch. God made us sexual creatures, and I praised him daily for that blessing. And I'd continue to do so until it was time to settle down, and I was definitely too young for that now.

I found solace in knowing that I was only invested for one night. It was far more appealing than my heart getting involved. I wasn't interested in getting hurt or being responsible for someone else's feelings. Growing up in boarding schools with parents who'd rarely called, I simply hadn't developed the skill necessary for sympathy or empathy... and maybe I'd missed the ones for settling down as well. With a degree in psychology, one would think I'd have sorted all that out long before now, but I'd never really been interested in analyzing myself.

Gabby groaned, and I realized I'd spent the entire ride completely zoned out. "Oh my God. Of course, there's no parking."

She stopped in front of the club like a spot

might materialize if she hoped for it hard enough. The sidewalk was packed, and there was a line out the door and down the block to get in. Right Nine was one of the most popular spots in town. It wasn't quite high-end, although it didn't attract the kind of people I didn't want to spend a night with, either. Riley and I made appearances here a couple times a month. Not often enough to be considered regulars, but frequently enough that the bouncers let us in ahead of the crowd. With our appearance came a slew of cameras and attention that the club ate up. As soon as someone tagged us on social media that line wouldn't just be down the block, the bouncers would be handpicking who got inside.

By the time the night was over, our appearance here would have made everyone inside a tidy sum in tips. It didn't hurt that my father owned this bar and most of the other popular ones in the area. He'd made millions in nightlife investments following a pretty stellar pro-basketball career. My fame had come from his name, but whatever. It was what it was, and I loved the life I led.

"Just valet." I shrugged, unsure of why this

was even a question. It would be comped, so I wasn't certain why she cared.

She eyed me with the gaze of a girl who hadn't grown up with a silver spoon in her mouth. Every time we came, the two of us had the same argument. Gabby and Riley wanted to pay the tab, and I thought we should take advantage of the perks that came with the territory.

I let out a frustrated huff and shifted uncomfortably in the seat—this dress was not made for sitting. "Look around, Gabs. You can either valet, or we can walk a mile. Up to you."

Reluctantly, she pulled into the line, and a guy about fell over himself trying to help her out of the car. Clearly a newbie, but he was cute—and way too young. He might have had a chance with Riley, but he'd picked the wrong chick in the terrific trio. I rolled my eyes and took the hand of the gentleman who'd opened my door. Silently, I thanked God for the reprieve—much longer in that position in that car and I would have passed out from the squeeze of my dress.

With Riley on my right and Gabby on my left, the three of us walked right past the line and straight to the door with our shoulders back and our heads high. They didn't own the status the way I did, but when we all got together, the air just crackled. Women glared with jealousy, and men craned their necks to get the best look possible.

And just when the bouncer opened the door to let us pass, a girl in line jumped up and down with excitement. "They're here."

I didn't bother to look back to see her friend's reaction. I was quite certain she was green with envy. They all were.

The three of us crossed the threshold into darkness. Music pumped around us, shaking the floor with bass, and the dim, blue light played off the purple of my silky dress. It took a minute for my eyes to adjust, but once they had, I noticed the latest addition. Machines created fog at the ceiling that fell and dissipated into the crowd on the dance floor. My father was a pro at creating a dynamic nightlife. People loved him and his clubs.

Riley motioned toward the bar, and Gabby and I followed to grab drinks. The bartender recognized us—wisely—and put our tab on my father's account. I always rewarded the employees who remembered us without asking. Hefty tips seemed to grab people's attention. With the majority of the customers out on the floor, finding a table had been an easy task. Sitting, however, was not. This dress caused more issues than I cared to admit. Nevertheless, I would endure. Beauty was pain.

Each of us took turns sliding into the leather lounge that was more like a couch with a tiny table in front of it than a booth, and I sipped at my amaretto sour to numb the pain of my shoes and this dress.

"There are way too many choices." Riley grinned over the edge of her glass, referring to what she assumed were eligible men.

I nodded, although I hadn't locked in on anyone in particular that caught my eye. Gabby wore the same smug expression she always did in these circumstances. She thought she'd won because she'd nabbed the good-looking doctor, but James still equaled commitment, regardless of the letters after his last name or the digits in his bank account.

Riley's attention had stopped, but I hadn't figured out who had stopped it.

"Which one?" Gabby twirled her straw,

mixing her drink. She might not be interested in taking anyone home, but she loved playing the games with us. More times than not, she found the lucky bachelor who got Riley or me for the night.

But there was a method to the madness. They had to be hot, no visible signs of attachment—wedding rings were not attractive, and neither were cheaters—and they couldn't be someone Mommy and Daddy would be proud to have show up for Christmas dinner. The point in a one-night stand was just that—one night. Blue-collar men made my body sing, but I'd never consider one for a life mate. And so, slumming it made this easy. We didn't go after guys in our social circle, and anyone who got chosen only got chosen once. One and done. In and out. Guys did it all the time, and I wouldn't apologize for having a good time.

Riley angled her cup in the direction of a guy in an attempt to remain unfazed. The blond made eye contact at that moment and tipped his beer in the air in acknowledgment. Anyone else would have cowered in the corner in embarrassment. Not Riley.

Gabby homed in on him. "Twenty bucks

says he's a mechanic." She lifted her drink to her lips.

I'd never know how she did it, but she was usually right. "How would you know that?"

The guy was certainly fit, but not overly so, and his eyes were what made him so alluring. Even from here, I could tell they were a pale green or blue, and coupled with his tanned skin, they stood out.

"Stains on his fingers." Gabby scrunched her brow as if it were obvious.

"How the hell can you see that from here? Are you a damn eagle?" I tossed back the last of my drink and flagged a waitress down for another.

Riley balked at the two of us bantering back and forth. "Ladies. Focus."

"Go talk to him." I nudged her gently with my shoulder. We weren't in high school, and I wouldn't make an issue out of a guy flirting with her; she'd move when she was ready.

I, on the other hand, wasn't anywhere near as bold as my friend. I didn't just go up to a guy and tell him that I wanted a night with him. First of all, that was tacky. Secondly, there was an art to seduction. I believed a man should make the first move if he wanted my attention—not that I wouldn't encourage him, but I just wasn't quite as brazen as Riley. And I certainly wasn't going to chase down someone lucky to grace my bed in the first place.

She took another sip of her drink, licked her lips, and then set down her glass with nothing remaining but ice cubes. "Order me another. I may or may not be back to drink it."

I nearly choked on the alcohol the waitress had brought back when Riley adjusted her breasts in her dress. Gabby and I laughed with encouraging words and watched as she strutted —and she did strut—across the floor.

The waitress we'd had was nowhere in sight, and I wasn't interested in sitting around, hoping another drink would magically appear. "You want another drink?" Three would be my limit, but I needed to slow down, or the third one would knock me on my ass before I even set my sights on an eligible bachelor for the evening.

Gabby held up her glass to show me she hadn't finished the first one. Thank God she remembered she was the DD. I finished my second drink and got up to get another round.

The bar was crowded, and it would only get worse. People snapped pictures—that I imagined were headed for social media—as I passed. And when I reached the swarm four people deep to place an order, I wiggled my way up to the bartender.

The group folded back in around me, although one in particular pressed against my back. There was zero excuse for anyone to ever invade my personal space like that. My shoulders went tight as I leaned farther over the bar, trying to get Brock's attention, not wanting to turn around. I couldn't tell who it was, only that after a moment, the smell of alcohol was muddled by a woodsy cologne that was absolutely—

A deep voice cut through my thoughts. "Sorry miss, I didn't see you there—"

Delicious.

Chapter Two

I probably should have placed some stipulations on going out. We typically did low key, but for some reason, I'd let Nick talk me into some hotshot bar—Right Nine, whatever that meant—that managed to attract the fucking paparazzi. I couldn't even think of anyone who lived in this town worth photographing, much less following to do it.

The place was packed, there was fucking fog coming from the ceiling, and blue lights flashed like the cops on the scene of an accident. I couldn't go one foot without being stepped on or bumped into, and all I wanted to do was get a fucking beer from the bar before the DJ played another pop song that made me want to stab myself in the eardrum with an icepick. I'd just about given up—prepared to snatch my best friend up by the scruff of the neck and drag his ass out of here—when I saw her.

In a crowd of bodies, her pert ass drew—and held—my attention. On instinct, I licked my lips and set my sights. She moved like she owned the place, and my guess was it wouldn't have taken much for her to stake her claim here.

She wiggled her way through the swarm of people and leaned over the bar where she patiently waited her turn. I moved closer on my own accord, no longer caring who got in my way. I was a stout guy who didn't take shit from anyone and intimidated most. I slid in behind her, close enough to catch a whiff of her floral perfume. It filled my nostrils, eliminating the stench of alcohol and musk of vape. It wasn't roses, but nevertheless, it was the nicest thing I'd smelled in a long-ass time. But with where I worked, that was no surprise.

Her spine stiffened, and her shoulders visibly tensed as if she'd sensed my arrival but couldn't identify what she'd noticed. She stiffened at the sound of my voice and then quickly turned. She was several inches shorter than me, even in heels. I smirked at the surprise marking her big, brown eyes that widened the longer she stared. When she finally blinked, it set off a chain reaction: she tossed her long, light-brown hair over her shoulder, licked her lips, and pushed out her chest.

My eyes darted down to her full breasts and perfect cleavage, fighting the neckline of her dress. That deep purple set off her tanned skin, and made her look edible—like a grape but not round...just tasty. I didn't even like grapes; I just knew I wanted to sample her. "Can I get you a drink?" My birthday aside, I'd buy her all the drinks she wanted.

She smiled innocently enough, but there was a mischievous gleam in her eyes that I couldn't quite identify. Princess mentality maybe. "I'm here with friends." She tugged her glossy bottom lip between her teeth and then let it slip out with a bit of a pop. This girl was good. She knew exactly what she was doing and just how crazy she made the opposite sex.

I was every bit as confident and not at all

intimidated. "I could be persuaded into buying a round for them as well."

The woman waited for what I wanted to barter. Her confidence went beyond knowing she looked good to an air of superiority. She did an appraisal of her own and arched a brow.

"In exchange for a dance. With you."

I took her nod to be an agreement and waved down the bartender with little effort. She huffed at the ease in which I'd gotten his attention but placed her and her friends' order anyhow. With her drinks and my beer in hand, I allowed her to lead the way to her table. Each step she took garnered my full attention, but it wasn't her feet I watched sway underneath that dress. I was an ass man, and hers was fucking perfect. Not a damn thing jiggled anywhere on her tight little frame.

She motioned for me to set down the drinks, and then turned to her friends—yup, definitely a princess, which worked out fine for me. Once she found out what I did for a living and realized I wouldn't raise her net worth, she'd be out the door faster than I could toss the condom in the trash. The rock on her friend's hand only gave me further confirmation.

"I'm going to dance." She didn't introduce us, and I didn't introduce myself.

They met my grin with an appraisal of their own. I wasn't stupid. They were sizing me up the way men did women. It was a two-way street regardless of how women liked to pretend it was offensive. The only ones who were offended by an appraisal were those who didn't fare well in the end. Basically, the ugly ones. Gorgeous girls never had a problem with men staring—they ate that shit up as long as it didn't get creepy. These two were hot, they knew it, and they smiled at her, having non-verbally given her their okay. I'd seen those interactions before, and I'd always done well in the friend-meet-hook-up process.

I took her hand, this stranger's, and her warm palm was covered by mine. Our fingers intertwined, and we were swallowed by the crowd. When she settled on a spot on the dance floor, I pulled her closer by her hips. Her frame was small but meaty. Either she worked out or had been blessed with genes she could charge a fortune to clone. Her front met mine, and I stared down my nose at the space between us. I didn't have a damn clue how either of our bodies moved, just that her tiny hands had landed on my biceps, and she seemed to like what she'd found.

I had to lean down to shout near her ear; otherwise, she wouldn't have heard me. "I'm Carter."

She pulled back, licked her lips, and then tugged on my neck, bringing my ear to her mouth. "Brayleigh." The heat of her name on my skin brought images to mind that rivaled the best porn I'd ever seen, and it all starred her.

I stood straight and mouthed her name, grinning at her. My hands slipped from her waist to her back and all the bare skin her dress left uncovered. The beat pumped, we danced, and I thought about what a great fucking birthday this had turned out to be. I'd have to thank Nick wherever he was. I didn't even care.

All I knew was that tonight I'd been destined to meet Brayleigh, and nothing said happy birthday like a one-night stand with an elite chick. I could tell by looking at her, she wasn't the fireman's girlfriend type, which worked out perfectly because this fireman wasn't looking for a girlfriend. Just a night.

Chapter Three

There wasn't a soft edge to this guy. My body was flush with a wall of solid muscles and hard planes. His muscles had muscle, and it was sexy as hell. I'd lost myself in how he felt and smelled, barely paying attention to the beat of the music. The closest I came to rhythm was following the heavy hands that rode low on my hips and the clear-blue eyes that trapped me in their lust-filled gaze. This man was hot as hell—Carter—I thought of his name and wanted to be moaning it instead.

He leaned down and spoke into my ear. "I like the way you move." The depth of his voice rattled inside me, sending a shiver down my spine and a quake between my legs.

I'd only had two drinks, but I was woozy with arousal. I pulled back and grinned. If he liked the way I rolled my hips to the sway of the music, all he had to do was turn on the radio, and I'd show him just how incredible my dancing could be. This wasn't my first rodeo, and I didn't plan to give in so easily.

"You want to get a drink?" He motioned toward my table and the alcohol we'd left sitting there.

The smolder on his face rushed to my already heated skin, pushing me to the limit. I wasn't typically bold, and I certainly never made the first move. But something about him affected me, lit me on fire, sparked a flame inside my loins that alcohol would only intensify—and it wasn't love at first sight. In that moment, only one thing seemed to matter.

I wrapped my arms tightly around his waist and peered up at him. I'd seen how he reacted when I licked my lips, and he liked it best when I pulled one between my teeth. It was coy. It would also get me what I wanted. "How about we get out of here instead?"

He didn't miss a beat before he nodded and jerked his head toward the exit. I inhaled sharply, catching a whiff of his delicious, woodsy scent. It was more than cologne or aftershave, but whatever it was, I couldn't place it. With his hand in mine, I tugged him through the crowd. Gabby and Riley were dancing with guys I'd never met near the table we'd had earlier. I motioned for Carter to give me a second and went to tell my friends I was leaving.

I hugged them both goodbye but not before turning on my location so they could track me from their iPhones—at least they'd know where to collect the body if this guy turned out to be the next Charles Manson. I shook off that sideways notion and returned to Carter's side.

He'd waited patiently, and when I was within reach, he extended his hand. He held on tight and acted as a linebacker between me and the front door. Carter was quite effective at clearing a path, although it didn't hurt that women parted so they could stare at him, and men moved because he was enormous.

He was a sight to behold from the front, but he sure as hell wasn't shabby from behind. His broad shoulders gave him girth, and while his arms were thick, they weren't so meaty that they bulged out from his sides. It was clear he worked out, that he was fit. And damn, his narrow waist was rock solid and trim, and I could only imagine how chiseled his abs would look based on how they felt. There wasn't an inch of this man that could possibly disappoint—or there better not be an inch. I needed at least eight and preferred nine. A small dick on this giant would not do. I expected to be worked over, and he'd need a sizeable member to handle that task—God help us both if he couldn't work it.

Carter stopped near the front to talk to some guy shooting darts—another add-on my dad hadn't shared with me—with a heavy-set, redhead. The skater guy kept his hand firmly planted on her plump ass the entire time the two men talked. Then his friend glanced at me, smirked, and shouted happy birthday to Carter.

I had no idea it was his special day—not that I would have. It wasn't like we were close. "It's your birthday?" Although, I could make his wish come true, and if he had a ribbon, I'd gladly tie myself up with a bow for him to unwrap.

We cleared the exit and stepped out into

the cool night air. Carter held me to his side at the waist as we walked down the narrow alley toward where I assumed he'd parked. My judgment clearly wasn't at its best since I was currently leaving the safety of Right Nine with a guy I didn't know, walking down a dark alley.

He shrugged. "Yeah, the big two-seven." As if that weren't a big deal.

I wrapped my other arm around his waist and ignored the burn my heels gave me as we walked. "Happy birthday. I would have bought you a drink if I'd known." *Or my dad would have. Details.*

"No worries." His fingers squeezed into my hips with a familiarity that shouldn't have been there—like he knew just where to touch to turn me on effortlessly. "The dance was perfect."

Soon enough, he stopped at a sleek, black truck—it was as masculine as he was—that I quickly learned belonged to Carter. Like a gentleman, he extended his hand to help me inside. The tanned leather cooled my bare thighs, and I took a quick look around before he joined me on the other side. He glanced at me as he revved the engine, then let his eyes roam over my body before they settled back on mine.

"You are so damn sexy." The smirk that lifted the corner of his mouth made me want to give him a present here in the truck.

I smiled and accepted the compliment he offered. "You're not too shabby yourself." I wasn't one of those girls to deny the truth, and there wasn't a single part of me that believed he would have said it if he hadn't meant it. There was no need for flattery when he was already going to get laid.

As he pulled out of the parking lot, I checked the group chat with Gabby and Riley. They'd both given Carter two thumbs up but still told me to be safe and not to exchange phone numbers. I didn't try to hide my smile when I responded. I believed in intuition, sixth senses, and bad feelings, and I heeded that nag in the pit of my stomach when and if it ever reared its head. So far it had served me well, but it appeared to have taken tonight off. Carter gave off nothing but the right vibes.

THE DOOR HAD BARELY CLOSED BEHIND Carter when his mouth met mine in an intense exchange that I didn't hesitate to deepen. I'd waited all night to feel his lips. He tasted like beer and honey as our tongues swirled, driving an electric heat right down to my pussy. I ground against his leg, hoping he'd take the hint and take control.

His large hands circled my hips and lifted me up with ease. The fabric of my dressed inched up my thighs until it bunched at my waist, and I wrapped my legs around him. He hadn't broken the kiss, and I hadn't bothered to open my eyes. It was his house, and I expected he knew where he was taking me when he carried me down the hall.

Effortlessly, he placed me onto a soft surface, and I parted my lids when I realized I was no longer in the safety of his strong arms. I'd found myself firmly planted on his bed. I took in the dark sheets and matching grey décor. The carpet was almost black as were his walls. It was all incredibly masculine as was the man that stood in front of me.

He took the liberty of removing his shirt, and I took off my shoes. As my heels hit the floor, my eyes traveled from the deep *V* of his Adonis belt to the midline down the center of his six-pack, except upon actual count, there were eight. His pecs were broad and raised from his chest, and his arms were perfect. His biceps contracted as he crawled onto the bed where he hovered between my legs. Our eyes met in an intense gaze before his lips descended upon mine. Nipping, sucking. The perfect blend of tongue and teeth teased with spice and heat. Carter kissed like an absolute God, and I now had proof that he looked like one too.

I laced my fingers through his hair to control how far he went, and where his body was hard, his short hair was soft. Once I'd stilled his head, his hands began to roam. They explored my body, drawing up from my thighs to my waist. Heated skin on burning flesh was even better when there was nothing left between us, and he'd stripped away my dress. I'd been confined by that thing all night, and for the first time since I'd left my penthouse, I felt free—uninhibited.

He eased back, appraising—or maybe memorizing—my body with those bright-blue eyes of his, setting me aflame. It was one of those moments where I wished I knew more about him—what he did, what he liked—but the notion passed as quickly as it came. I'd never cared where they spent their time or their money as long as they looked respectable and fucked like a slut. Not that I did this weekly or even monthly. It had been almost six months since I'd last hooked up with anyone, but when I had an itch, I wanted it scratched. Carter could satisfy that need, then I'd forget that I'd ever wondered about his career or his friends, and I'd go back to being Brayleigh.

Leaning over me, he kissed down the center of my chest to the swell of my breasts until he reached the cup of my bra. His hand came around me, undoing it with just the flick of his fingers and then drawing it down my arms. And in the same breath, he slid my panties from my legs, and I was completely exposed.

A growl started deep in his chest as he trailed his pointed finger down my waxed pussy. "Damn," he murmured and leaned in close, kissing my navel as his gaze bored into mine. He held my eyes when he slipped his finger between my folds.

I smirked. "Aren't you going to eat your birthday cake?" I wiggled my hips, and each move sent him closer to where I wanted him to be.

Carter didn't answer with words. Instead, he slid two fingers in deep, the sound of my arousal filling the silent room. My back arched off the bed, and my mind spun with the ceiling fan as his thumb circled my clit. The pad of his finger did the work until the warmth of his lips kissed my hot flesh.

I let out a garbled moan and pushed my hips toward him, spreading my legs wide. I laced my fingers in his hair and was prepared to hold him there as long as I saw fit. Carter was so fucking good.

His fingers worked my G-spot inside while his tongue caressed my slit and clit. Just as I would near the edge, he'd release the suction on my tiny pearl and slather his tongue between my lips. I had no idea what pattern he followed or what trick would come next. All I was certain of was my name, and I had started to question that. He hooked his fingers, massaging my clit. There wasn't one he worked more than the other—the two built in tandem as I began to gush. I felt full and pressured at the same time, the desire building until it bubbled at the surface.

I moaned so deeply that the sound came from my chest. "Carter, don't fucking stop." My nipples pebbled, and I pinched and tweaked them as Carter continued the ministration between my legs, devouring my pussy. It was divine and sinful.

He didn't stop to respond, and I almost missed the gleam in his eyes that resulted from the smirk on his face as he watched me circle my peaks. There was something hedonistic about watching a man eat my pussy, making eye contact with him as I ground my cunt on his face, riding his mouth. His blue eyes grew darker as he went, and I noticed the slightest pulse of his pupils every time he breathed in my scent.

The tremors started inside, building in intensity. It was a roll I wouldn't be able to stop once it started. His hands gripped my thighs, pressing them to the bed, keeping me wide and open as he used his mouth to focus on me. My most sensitive spot was lavished with attention. I was done for. I erupted in the most delicious orgasm I may have ever had. Wracked with spasmatic pleasure, I rode out the storm, relishing in the way it consumed my body.

"Jesus...that was amazing." I gasped, trying to catch my breath.

Carter licked his way back up my body. "I'm not even close to being done with you yet." He placed a wet kiss against the center of my breast, right above my nipple, before his tongue trailed down to suckle me.

I writhed against him at how good it felt, and my pussy started to pulse again. My whole body wanted more. More of this. More of Carter. Just, *more*. His jeans still hung low on his hips, and I desperately wanted him naked. Reaching down to the waistband, my knuckles grazed the thin hairs of his happy trail. With little effort, I unbuttoned his jeans and shoved them down along with his boxer briefs. He kicked them off, and his hard cock hit my inner thigh. His mouth alternated between each of my nipples as I wrapped my hand around him or jeez—tried to. He was *hung*.

My fingers didn't meet as I stroked him, but Carter didn't seem to mind. The noises that came from deep in his chest spurred me on. He rolled to his side and let me play. I used the pad of my thumb to cover his head in the thick lubricant he produced, and when my palm slipped over the head, circling back down, his hips bucked. The flick of my tongue over the brim of his cock had him shuddering and his skin erupting in noticeable pleasure. But I wanted to do more than just tease. I wanted to taste. My lips parted, and I slid his head into my mouth. My tongue lavished his dick with attention while I took him, inch by inch until he hit the back of my throat.

"Fuck." He pulled away and cupped my jaw. There was something in his eyes besides lust, although it wasn't something I identified before he got up. Carter fumbled around the drawer of his nightstand to find a condom.

I took the foil packet when he climbed back onto the bed and tore it open with my teeth. He straddled my chest with his cock in my face. I stared up at him through the haze of a drink or two, but if there were ever a time I knew what I was doing, this was it. I was aware of every detail between the two of us, and I committed each one to memory. He was so fucking gorgeous and sexy, and I wasn't certain I'd ever seen a more visually captivating man. Carter even held my attention when he took the unwrapped condom, and I watched him roll it down the length of his thick shaft. I couldn't help but wonder where the hell he planned to put that thing.

"Like what you see?" He winked, and I melted. Then he grabbed my hips and slid me farther down the bed, hanging my ankles on his shoulders. *Oh my...*

"Mhm." Everything about this moment was perfect, and I was elated.

This was the perfection God had blessed people to share. Together.

The head of his large cock slid through my wetness, nudging my throbbing clit. My pussy clenched, desperate for the fullness only Carter's cock could provide. And Jesus what I wouldn't give to have him inside me, right now.

I couldn't stop the gasp that passed my lips when he entered me, stealing my breath. It took me a second to realize that Carter had only gone halfway. But I wanted more. I needed more. I wanted it all. My greedy cunt wanted his massive cock. It took some maneuvering, but with each wiggle of my hips, he brought me closer until his thighs were pressed against my ass, and nothing separated us.

Carter gripped my knees and used them as leverage. He drove into me with such force the bed moved. My breasts jostled, and our skin slapped. It was deep and rough and perfect. The sound of his name rang through the air over and over before I realized it was me that moaned it, maybe even screamed it. This man knew what he was doing, and for a split second, I wondered if his career were porn. But the second his thumb circled over my exposed clit, that notion flew from my mind along with everything else. One hand drew the answers to life on my pussy while the other roamed my body. Yet regardless of where his palms were or what his fingers did, he never stopped driving into me. Carter had guaranteed I'd remember his name tomorrow, and there was no doubt, I'd be thinking about him every time I took a step. He'd branded my body with his own style of fucking, and it was one I'd have a hard time recovering from.

Our bodies glistened with a sheen of sweat —although he'd done all the work—and I hovered on the edge of another orgasm. My clit throbbed, desperate for another release. I reached down and rubbed myself to the edge, massaging my hot flesh until I came apart. The climax pulsed through my veins and then my body, each pounding pulse like a drum I heard in my ears and felt in my limbs. And when the clenching of my pussy slowed and the throbbing of my pulse quieted, Carter slowed, stilled, and came. Each spasm of his cock was like an earthquake inside me, and his body tensed in time with his release.

He covered my frame, careful to hold his weight on his forearms. There he lavished me with an intense kiss that felt far more personal than erotic, even though it was breathless. When Carter slid out of me, I mewled at the loss. But my heart sang when he pulled back and offered me a cocky smirk and a wink.

"I think there should be more than one round of birthday sex."

I'd give him an orgasm for every year he'd be alive if that's what the man wanted.

Chapter Four

If it were up to me, I would be in deep all night. And I was right. Brayleigh was as insatiable as I was, so as soon as I recovered, I was all over her again. She made no bones about the fact that she loved sex, and I loved a woman who took what she wanted without apology.

Brayleigh was damn near perfect, and I'd explored just about every inch of her. The skin on her neck erupted into chills as my lips made their way from behind her ear to the dip between her clavicles. She tilted her head back to give me better access while trailing her hands up my arms and over to my pecs. It was a lazy exploration that she enjoyed while I feasted on her until she reached my hardening cock. Her hand didn't quite fit around my girth, but she didn't have any problem pumping me. My excitement grew in her palm, and I became almost delirious at her touch.

My body hovered over hers as I stared into her soft, brown eyes. I held her stare until my lids closed and our mouths met. My tongue lapped at hers, and we both fought for the upper hand. As the intensity of the kiss grew, I ran my hand down the curve of her ass and gripped her firm globe. She broke the kiss and moaned against my mouth in response.

"Turn over, Brayleigh," I whispered into her ear, and a sly smile spread across her full lips when I pulled away.

I pushed myself up while she flipped over. Snagging another condom from my drawer, I opened it with my teeth, and then rolled it on. Fuck she was gorgeous. Brayleigh watched me over her shoulder. When her eyes dropped to my dick, her nostrils flared just slightly, and I couldn't wait to get inside her. This girl wanted me as badly as I did her, and she didn't bother hiding it. She wasn't doing me a favor or *letting* me have my way with her. Brayleigh was all in.

My gaze dropped to her cinched waist and her round hips as I grabbed them, and I pulled her onto her knees. She knew the drill. Head down, ass up. In seconds, she'd pushed forward on her forearms, popping her luscious ass into the air. I nearly lost it when she then situated her feet, spreading them, and her pussy was slick with desire. There was nothing I wanted more than to slam into her tight cunt right then, but two strokes and I'd be out. I needed more. I tried to quell my desire and still my racing heart, but touching Brayleigh in any way did nothing to quench my lust. Nevertheless, I drew out the anticipation for her and ran my hands up her inner thighs. She trembled, and her low moan lingered in the room.

I licked my lips and watched her pussy glisten like I was in a damn trance. With my dick in hand, I pushed my hips forward and slid my head through her wet folds and around her swollen clit. The more she moaned, the longer I'd do it. Every sound she made drove me forward. I could fuck this woman for the next two days and only get up to piss and eat. Her pussy was that fucking addictive.

"Carter..." she whined and then begged, "fuck me. *Hard*."

There was a tiny sigh at the end that was breathless and wanton. It went straight to my cock. My dick jumped like it had been beckoned, and I impaled her in one thrust.

If it were possible to get lost in a chick's pussy, I was fairly certain I'd gone so far into Brayleigh's that I wouldn't be finding my way out. She was just so fucking tight in the most perfect of ways. Instead of fighting it, I shut my eyes and surrendered to the loss of control. The two of us were completely in tune physically—her body and mine spoke their own language. She took every thrust, meeting me ass for hip. Skin slapping echoed in the room, and grunts matched the claps. Every forward motion went farther than the last.

My fingertips dug into the soft skin that surrounded her hips the closer I got. It was hot, intense, primal—feral—just like I liked it. Brayleigh fucked effortlessly as if we'd choreographed a dance ahead of time, and she'd memorized her part. She rotated her hips with each backward drive in a way that caught the head of my dick where it was most sensitive...

every time. Yet somehow, she managed to take me right up to the edge and pull me back.

"Shit," I murmured to myself and repositioned us.

Brayleigh moved back, practically straddling my thighs when I rocked onto my haunches. That minor adjustment took me deeper inside her tiny frame, and it gave me unrestricted access to her front. I splayed my hands across her chest, caressing her full breasts, almost holding her up as she rode my cock in a modified reverse cowboy. I leaned forward, my lips at her spine, and as I inhaled the intoxicating scent of her shampoo, her soft curls bounced against my chest. I spread my thighs a bit wider, taking her weight while she rode my cock in the best birthday fuck I'd ever received.

She leaned back and wound her arms around my neck. A loud moan rang in my ear when the adjustment hit her deep inside at a place that made her weak. I wrapped my forearm across her hips and the other across her chest to use her shoulder for leverage. Her body curved in the softest, most supple lines, and I wished I could have kissed every inch of her tanned skin while continuing to make her pussy clench. Her heat began to rise, and I didn't stand a chance. I circled her clit with my finger and took her over the edge with me.

She pulsed and gushed, and the fruits of our exchange ran down my balls as I came. I didn't have a clue if it was her arousal or my come, not that I cared. It was fucking hot. I eased her forward onto the mattress as I pumped the last of my release into her and then fell to her side.

Her eyes met mine, and I kissed her lips. Our tongues swirled together languidly. The taste of sweet liquor still lingered along with a hint of mint. I cupped her jaw in my hand and laced my fingers through her hair as she draped her thigh over my hip. Somehow, she managed to rock back over my cock.

"Fuck, Brayleigh," I groaned into her mouth. "You're killing me." I moved her off me, laying her on her back as she laughed. "Death by sex. I guess if I have to go, that's the way to do it." I tossed the second condom and found a third. I was far from done.

I settled between her legs when I got back on

the bed. I'd need a bit to recover, but that didn't mean I couldn't continue to enjoy her body in the meantime. My lips returned to hers, and she wrapped her arms around the nape of my neck as she lost herself in the kiss. The sting of her nails over my shoulders became an exquisite pleasure. My arms shook from the strain of holding myself and her up. Carefully, I lowered my body, staying on my elbows. Her breast filled my large hands, and her nipples puckered at my touch. An erotic moan rumbled in her chest when I pinched her peaks, rolling the pale-pink buds.

"That feels good, Carter."

I didn't need her confirmation—her body gave her away—but I still liked hearing it. Every guy wanted to know he'd pleased the woman he was with; otherwise, he'd failed at what he was doing. There was also something sexy as fuck about a woman who could communicate what she liked.

She reached down and took my semi-hard cock in her hands, stroking me back to full mast. It was the way she flicked my tip where I was most sensitive and had the right pressure around my shaft that kept bringing my dick back to life. I felt the desire down in my spine, maybe all the way to my toes.

I rolled off Brayleigh and onto my back as I put on the condom. When I gave her my attention again, she smirked and kicked her leg over me to straddle my waist.

"I should treat the birthday boy to a ride, right?" A devilish gleam sparkled in her eyes, and I grinned back.

I nodded. "Yes, ma'am." Her thighs were warm when I slid my hands up from her knees to her hips and then guided her over my cock.

She was as hungry for me as I was for her, riding me like she had to have my dick to breathe and she'd been fighting for air. I simply couldn't get enough of her. Her pussy gripped my shaft, and the heat of her cunt was heaven. Every time she rolled her hips and came down, I fought not to shoot my load. I tried to set the pace by encouraging her ass with my hands, but she wasn't having it.

Brayleigh's hands splayed over my chest to hold herself steady felt like anchors. She arched her back, causing her hair to fall over her shoulders. The sway of her locks over her pert tits as she rode me was intoxicating. I could get drunk watching this chick fuck me. The way she moaned was so uninhibited and natural that I hung onto every breathless noise, but it was the way my name left her tongue and parted her lips that did something to me emotionally. I ignored that tug in favor of focusing on meeting her body with mine. I couldn't get deep enough to satisfy the urge.

It was way too easy to connect with her, but I had to fight the temptation. The pull for something more nagged at my thoughts, but I knew I had to spare myself the line. Trying to see her again was an impossibility. I didn't do more than one night. No strings. Ever. I'd enjoy this and be done with it—but damn—with the way she worked me.... I wouldn't forget about her.

When I couldn't stave off the climax any longer, I growled through gritted teeth. "Fucking hell...."

She laid on my chest as she came with me, her pussy choking my cock with the beat of her orgasm. Her entire body was consumed with the aftermath, and I wrapped my arms around her lower back and held her close as she came down. Neither of us moved as we caught our breath, and it wasn't until I couldn't stand the feel of the used condom any longer that I moved to get up.

"Where's your bathroom?" Her voice was softer than I'd noticed at the club, sweeter and far more feminine.

"Through there." I pointed to the door I'd just come through after tossing the rubber and laid back down.

She grabbed my shirt from the floor and waltzed into the bathroom. I grinned at how easy it was to be with her and how comfortable Brayleigh was in my home...until I acknowledged what that meant, and then I quickly dismissed the thought altogether.

My phone dinged, and I tugged on a pair of boxer briefs when I got up to check it. By the time I'd responded to the text message and turned back the sheets, Brayleigh waltzed out of the bathroom. She was quiet as a ninja and as light on her feet as a dancer. She stood at the edge of the bed with my T-shirt on. It swallowed her but tented at her still peeked nipples and stopped at her thighs. Part of me wanted to have her spin so I could see the crease of her ass at the hem.

"You can uh...stay if you want." I sounded less than convinced, and I wanted to slap the shit out of myself the moment the sentence came out of my mouth. I was quite certain she noticed.

She smiled, but it didn't reach her eyes. "That's okay. I'll just Uber home."

I nodded. I purposefully waited as she had gathered her things from around the room so I could see her perfect ass play peek-a-boo with the edge of my shirt. And then I got up and walked her to the door. It didn't dawn on me until she'd left that she'd worn my favorite shirt and boxer briefs out the door.

Waking up the next morning, my head pounded from dehydration, and my dick was hard with morning wood. One of those I was used to, and the other I could do without. I got up and went through my usual routine, hoping it would alleviate the headache. After I watched the news through a cup of coffee, I checked with the guys about our Saturday-morning workout. Most of the men at the station worked out every morning unless we were on duty. Brian was coming off a twenty-four-hour rotation, so I hadn't expected him to join us, but at the last minute, he decided he was in. The three of us, Nick, Brian, and I, had worked out together since the academy and had been best friends ever since. I didn't have siblings, so they were as close as it got.

Dressed in workout attire, I jumped into my truck and headed toward the gym. I likely just imagined things, but I would have sworn I could still smell Brayleigh's perfume in the cab. I smiled and banked those memories. Best piece of ass I'd ever had. But I hadn't managed to wipe the smirk from my face, and Nick noticed.

"Birthday sex to remember?" He chuckled.

"Fuck off. You looked like you were having a good time, too." We headed down to the locker room to secure our stuff, and as usual, Brian showed up late.

"Yeah, well, that's beside the point. You get her number?" Nick shook up his pre-workout drink, and I swigged at mine from my water bottle.

"Nah, one-time thing man." I shrugged.

"You know the drill. Plus, girls like that don't do guys like me long-term."

He gave me a funny look. "Okay..." It shouldn't come as a shock to him; I never got their numbers nor did I want them.

We walked out together and spotted Brian on his way in. He motioned that he was headed to the locker room, and we went into the gym, knowing he'd find us. The place was small, and we were usually the only ones in there except for a random person or two on a treadmill or elliptical.

"When is it *not* gonna be a one-time thing?" Nick had turned serious for the first time since I'd known him, and it stopped me in my tracks.

I didn't bother responding or even looking at him, though. He knew the answer to that question because he felt it himself—*never*. He huffed, shook his head, and kept walking when I refused to answer. There would never be a time when one night turned into two. That's just how it was.

"You two look like flat smoke." Brian grinned with his sunglasses on and strode across the room in his sweats and hoodie.

"We know how to have fun." I chuckled.

"Happy belated birthday, jackass. Sorry, I didn't get you a gift." He joked, not sorry at all.

We started on our workout, going our own way for the most part. The unit had a gym at the fire station, but we only used it when we were on shift. When you spent twenty-four solid hours at work, the last thing you wanted to do on your day off was show your face at the station. Plus, at the end of a grueling workout, we changed clothes and headed to the diner down the sidewalk for breakfast. We'd been doing this for nearly six years, and the routine never changed.

I sipped at my coffee after we'd taken a seat in our usual booth, staring down at the white, speckled table. Thoughts of last night kept crossing my mind, and I couldn't quiet them. I didn't have a ton of random encounters with women—a couple times a year maybe—but when I did, I never really thought about it after, and I certainly never thought about *them* after.

Our order came about the time Brian caught onto Nick's obnoxious line of question-ing. I was hungry as shit, so I chose to shovel food into my mouth instead of answering my best friend. But once the two of them started to tag team it, I took a gulp of coffee, swallowed, and retaliated.

"Why are you always bothering me about shacking up when you are still single yourself?" I laughed once, but I didn't find any of this shit even remotely funny.

Nick shrugged and grinned. "I'm waiting until thirty. I have a plan. You, however, don't." He explained what he believed made perfect sense, and in his mind, I'm sure it did, but to Brian and me, it was horseshit.

"Well, that's your business. You guys ready to go?" I asked.

My body was sore, I was exhausted, and I wanted to spend the rest of my day off doing absolutely nothing. My birthday always worked out that way. Both my folks were gone, so I didn't have much in terms of family and hadn't since I was nineteen. It wasn't until I met Nick and Brian that I really started to celebrate, and that was forced. It was also draining. Last year they had taken me to a strip club. Three girls had popped out of a cake, and three girls had gone home with me. This year our schedules were tougher with Brian on another shift, but it had still resulted in an all-nighter where I worked out until I could barely move a limb. I was beat and just wanted to get home.

"Yeah, let's get out of here."

We went our separate ways once we returned to the gym. Nick was probably just going to hit up one of his friends with benefits, and Brian would go home to Erica. I couldn't say there weren't times I didn't envy that because there were. Brian was able to juggle shit and make it work. But I couldn't be that guy.

My thoughts had ventured into dangerous territory, and I forced myself to veer off in another direction. But every route my thoughts took brought me back to the same brunette who'd ridden my cock with pride. I realized I might have to work to keep last night with Brayleigh out of my head.

Chapter Five

"Come on, Brayleigh, what was he like? Give me a little detail."

"Ugh, Riley...that would take all day." I sipped my ice water and poked at my brunch.

Gabby had just left us to get back to the hospital, and I was trying to recover from the alcohol I'd had last night. I'd only had a couple of drinks, but I paid the price today—or maybe it was the workout after the drinks to celebrate a certain someone's birthday.

"We have all day." She picked at her croissant and popped little pieces of the flaky crust into her mouth. "Last night was a bust. Let me at least live through your good time."

"You were talking to that guy when I left.

What happened?" The thought of food was more than I could stomach, but I knew if I didn't eat anything, I'd just feel worse.

Riley shook her head and finished chewing what was in her mouth. Her messy bun moved with her motion, and I was jealous of how cute she could look with zero effort. I'd opted for comfort over style and large sunglasses this morning, but it wasn't because it was cute.

She shrugged. "I don't know. He gave off some creepy vibes, and I just wasn't feeling it. Gabby and I danced for a bit, but we left shortly after you headed out. But you, girl, that dude was hot. What was his name?" Riley leaned in like she was about to hear some juicy gossip.

I didn't take the bait, nor did I dish out what she cared to hear. "I don't remember," I lied.

Riley nudged my knee under the table. "Yes, you do." She laughed, and I could tell by the gleam in her eye, she wouldn't let up.

It took very little to bring him to mind, and every time I thought of him, I couldn't stop my smile. "Carter. His name was Carter." I licked my lips as I pictured his eight-pack abs and ten-inch dick—it was an estimate, but I'd bet my trust fund I was right. And the next morning, I still felt the aftermath of a few naked hours with the birthday boy. I shifted in my seat for a reminder of the delicious bruising he'd left behind.

"Mhm. What does he do?" Riley tipped back her mimosa and motioned to the waitress for another; God, maybe I should start drinking again just to waste the day away.

I rolled my eyes and exhaled loudly. "I literally didn't ask him a single personal question. Like at all. It was just sex. A one-night stand I can forget about."

"I saw that man, Brayleigh. Lie to yourself all you want, but there is no forgetting *that*." Riley leaned back in her seat, continuing to pick at that damn croissant; I wanted to push the whole thing into her mouth and tell her to hush.

I didn't want to dwell on the fact that I couldn't get him out of my mind because I couldn't stop thinking about him long enough to acknowledge that a one-night stand meant just that. One night. I hadn't given him my number, and I certainly would not go by his house to ask him out. So, thinking about seeing him again was pointless. Unless happenstance got involved or he miraculously appeared at my door, Carter was a one-time gig...which sucked because everything with him had been easy: no awkward moments, no mishaps. There was an instant connection, and now I felt like I'd lost something. Mentally, I shrugged it off; losing great sex was always horrible.

"So you won't see him again, right?" Riley continued to press, and I wondered if she knew something I didn't. "I mean since you didn't get his number or anything." The waitress had brought her another mimosa, and she now sat in her seat with one arm folded over her lap and the other in front of her with that glass. She circled the stem between her fingers and held my eyes.

"Pretty unlikely. I didn't get the impression that he goes out a lot." I lifted my water to my lips and took another sip. "The only reason he was out last night was for his birthday."

Her nose scrunched, and her eyes narrowed. "Hmm."

I laughed uncomfortably at her odd behavior. "What is your deal?"

"Nothing." She held up her hands. "I'm just upset that you let that fine piece of ass go. He had to have been worth keeping nearby for a second go-around, right? Please tell me I'm right. Come on, Brayleigh, are you ever going to settle down?"

I rolled my eyes and wondered when Riley had started to talk like Gabby and my mom. "Oh God, you sound like my mother."

Every week my mom called to ask me the exact same things: How am I doing? How's work? When am I going to get a boyfriend? Two of those three answers remained the same every time she asked: Fine and never. My job was the only thing we ever spent any real time discussing, and that was because I loved it. I was a consultant for a non-profit organization that contracted me to work with other charities. Basically, I was an on-call psychologist for at-risk teens and young adults, primarily females. It didn't pay all that well, but I didn't need it to. I loved what I did. My parents, however, would prefer I play up the New York socialite scene. While that would be easier—and I'd had fun doing that in college—there was more to me than a pretty face and fat bank account. Most people just didn't know it.

"A girl's got to do what a girl's got to do. If that means playing the concerned mother figure in your life, then so be it. I worry about the stress of your job and the fact that you go home alone."

"Riley...you're single! What the hell?"

She shrugged and tossed back the last of her drink.

"Time to go. You've clearly had one too many mimosas, or you're starting to take after *your* mother and mixing alcohol with sedatives. Either one is not good."

Reluctantly, she stood after we paid the tab, and I tugged her out of the café. I made a mental note to start watching Riley's alcohol and pill consumption. This couldn't become a habit. Even if I didn't have proof that she'd actually done anything, she was acting strangely.

The two of us spent more time together than with Gabby. It wasn't because we didn't love Gabby, quite the opposite. Once she'd graduated from nursing school and started crazy night shifts, we just didn't see her much.

Then add in a fiancé, and it made things nearly impossible. Riley and I, on the other hand, both made our own schedules. She freelanced as a photographer, and we spent most of our spare time together. We kept Gabby in the loop through the group chat, but it just wasn't the same.

Today was no different. Gabby had gone to work on a new rotating shift, leaving Riley with me. And with a free Saturday and nothing to do, we'd decided to go to the nail salon. It followed brunch with ease, as would the massage we had booked later this afternoon.

She opened the door to the nail place and led me in. "How are your parents?" Riley loved my parents, and they loved her. Although now, I started to wonder if I needed to cut off her contact with my mom completely.

"They're fine. My dad asked me to come home for his birthday. He's celebrating in the Hamptons." We checked in with the receptionist and took a seat. "Maybe you can come? Otherwise, I don't want to go."

The girl at the front desk motioned that our chairs were ready, and Riley and I followed her back. I slid off my flipflops, climbed into the recliner, and put my feet in the hot water. By the time I got settled, I realized Riley hadn't responded. When I turned to look at her, she had a dopey grin on her face.

"Why not?" Her incredulous tone told me she had been talking to my mother. "It would be fun." She leaned back in the seat and put her head on the rest. "You haven't seen them in forever."

I gave her a side eye and wondered when she'd joined the enemy's team. "Fun? Hardly. My dad will just use it as an excuse to have his friends invite their single sons in an attempt to marry me off to someone with a mint account or a noble inheritance. Someone 'worthy of me.'" I used air quotes to illustrate my point. "It's exhausting, really."

"You sound like a brat."

"I agree." I snorted.

She was right. It was all pretentious and snobby, and while I liked to utilize my daddy's resources and didn't mind using his name to gain access and notoriety, I was not interested in a pre-arranged marriage or one of convenience.

"Good." She giggled. "Maybe I'll go and get

your dad to marry me off. I'd like one of those men who want to take care of a woman." She paused and appeared to think about what a life like that might look like. "Or, maybe I'll go out and find the mystery guy from last night." She waved her phone around, and I was inclined to toss it into the pedicure water.

I gasped, but not too loudly since there were other people in the salon. "Oh my God. No, you won't. I mean it, Riley." I laughed and hoped she understood.

I meant she couldn't go on a hunt for Carter—not that she couldn't get my dad to find her an eligible bachelor. I'd kill for just one photo of him, but I wouldn't admit that to her, preferably of his abs. Yes, his abs would have been nice memorabilia.

"Fine." She finally relented.

Riley promised not to mention Carter or the one-night stand again, but it wasn't her that I had to worry about. It was me that I'd have to continually remind to stop dwelling on a night that would never see a repeat.

I filled the following week. Every second of every day, I managed to keep occupied with work, meetings, and dinner dates with Riley and Gabby or both. But on Sunday evening, Riley had a photoshoot, and Gabby was on at the hospital, which left me alone. I was exhausted, and even though I didn't want time to myself, I relaxed in a hot bath while watching television. It was over the top, but baths were one of my favorite treats to give myself. And since I wasn't much of a leisure reader, I liked to binge on reality TV with a glass of wine from the tub.

For the most part, I lived a relatively stress-free life, but every once in a while, I needed to unwind. It was the outside pressures that built up and got to me—primarily my parents. My sister had married the guy my father would have picked for her the week after they'd both graduated from Princeton, so the nagging all fell on me. There was no one left to catch the flack—just me.

Once the water had cooled and I'd turned into a raisin, I got out and dried off. The plush, blue robe that I wrapped myself in felt like a warm hug after hanging on the towel warmer for an hour. My limbs were heavy, and my eyes stung, but it was far too early for bed. When I made my way to the living room, I lit a couple of candles for aromatherapy, grabbed a glass of wine, and watched TV there instead. One glass turned into three as the sappy Hallmark movie made me fantasize about a romantic reencounter with Carter that would never happen. It would have been a perfect Sunday night had I been able to keep my mind off the one thing I couldn't have. I set my wine on the coffee table next to a candle and laid down on my couch. The cushions welcomed me when I closed my eyes and remembered every detail of the best sex I'd ever had. My lids grew heavy as did my limbs. It was the last thing I remembered before I was asleep.

The stench of burned coffee filled my senses and rushed me awake. Except it wasn't coffee at all. An inferno of angry, orange flames cast across my fur rug and fanned out around the front door. I shot up from the couch faster than I should have given the alcohol intake and searched for my phone. I was dizzy by the time I found it on my nightstand, and the air was thick with smoke. I managed to dial the emergency numbers, but not much beyond slumping at my bedroom door—unable to move or catch my breath. I had to get up. I had to try to get out. The alarms blared in the building, and the electricity blinked and went out as I pulled myself up to the window.

With every last bit of energy I had, I tried to get the attention of the firemen on the grass below. I beat on the window, but I didn't have the strength to break the glass. My cry was muffled, and my throat stung.

And at some point, I passed out completely.

Chapter Six

I'd spent the last few days or so buried in work.

It wasn't like we were always out there fighting fires. We worked the training academy for the incoming trainees a few weeks out of the year. If 9-1-1 calls got dispatched to us for a possible fire, we still saddled up the rig to go. We were always busy. But it didn't deter the thoughts of Brayleigh that continued to run in my head even a week after I'd seen her.

We may not have said more than a hundred words to each other, but I actually wanted to talk to her, about whatever. I didn't know. Nick was still up my ass about finding her, not that there was much I could do about it. He was persistent—or obnoxious; however I wanted to spin it—that way.

"I have news." Brian came off the rig in half of his uniform.

The three of us stood in the bay, enjoying what little time we got to work together when we were at the academy. We spent a lot of hours waiting on something to happen, and sadly, filled it with gossip that would rival that of women.

A smug look passed Brian's face when he leaned against the wall. The shit-eating grin he sported indicated whatever he had to say was big news, so I folded my arms across my chest to wait, preparing myself for something epic or something overblown. I never knew which it would be with him.

Nick sucker punched him in the arm. "Are you going to tell us what it is, or are we going to spend the afternoon playing twenty questions?"

"Erica might be pregnant." Brian cheesed—like full-on, cheeks-touching-his-eyelashes grin, and Nick and I both said congrats at the same time.

"That's amazing. When did you find out?" I asked.

The goofy grin morphed into a more quizzical one, or maybe that was uncertainty. "I don't know for certain. But I'm pretty sure, well, at least we've been trying."

I chuckled; only Brian would be excited about his girlfriend being *possibly* pregnant. "So how do you know then?"

Brian had missed out on some critical reasoning skills somewhere along the way, but it was just part of what made him who he was. "Her boobs are bigger." His blank expression matched his monotonous tone. He really believed that meant Erika was pregnant.

I couldn't stop myself from clapping him on the shoulder with a chuckle. "Okay, man. Tell us when you have proof. And keep in mind, I call godfather." I didn't have a clue what I'd do with a kid, but if it were Brian's, I'd figure out a way to spoil it—God help that child if he had a girl.

Nick flicked his Powerade cap at Brian, who immediately tried to make it physical, tackling Nick at the knees. The two had no sooner started to roll around when the fire station alarm sounded, signaling a call. Nick and I were on-call, but Brian's crew was working equipment today.

"Reynolds and Burton, you're with us!" Our captain came in to snag Nick and me.

"See ya' on the flipside, Bri." I pulled my suspenders up as I took off toward the rig, grabbing my gear on the way.

In less than sixty seconds, the crew was on the engine, and we were rolling. We had a damn good team—fast and committed. And possibly, at times, a bit reckless. We got filled in on what the dispatcher knew as we rode. The address gave away the type of neighborhood—high class, fancy homes, rich people. But flames didn't discriminate. They didn't care what color you were or how much money you had in your bank account. Infernos took what they wanted despite the zip code.

"As far as we know, it hasn't spread past the top floor. Fifth-floor penthouse."

I listened intently and got into the head-space to do whatever needed to be done once we got there. I wasn't familiar with the building or the neighborhood really. We never knew what we were walking into, but knowing it was an apartment building limited our options. Add to it that the top floor—the one in flames—was one unit, and that meant there was likely no more than two doors in and out. The front and possibly a patio.

There were people gathered on the lawn in front of the building, and as we neared, it didn't appear the fire had spread to the lower levels, but it was just a matter of time. The left windows glowed a brilliant orange as flames beat the glass from the inside.

When we hopped out, the captain asked an onlooker for information. "Is there anyone inside?"

The guy shrugged. "There's a young girl that lives up there. Keeps to herself mostly." He looked around. "The rest of the tenants are out here. But I have no idea if she's even home."

Two of the guys went for the ladder, and I stared up at the building for just a second to try to get a layout in my head, a mental image to refer back to if I got inside and couldn't see through smoke and darkness. Just as I went to start pulling the rig, I noticed a figured in the window. But as quickly as I'd seen it, it had disappeared.

"There's someone inside," I hollered to my crew as they maneuvered the ladder.

Nick screamed back, "The swing arm's stuck. The ladder won't move."

Fuck. An equipment malfunction was the last thing we needed, but while Nick messed with the swing, I took off.

"Carter! What the hell are you doing?" Nick screamed as I headed into the burning building, pulling my helmet over my head as I went.

Nick was as tenured as I was, but the rest of the men on the ground, except for the Captain, weren't. While they dicked around trying to formulate a plan and two more engines pulled up, I took a risk that I knew better than to take. Firefighters should never go into a building alone. But when a life hung in the balance, the rules went out the window. I had no idea what would be on the other side of that door, but waiting for a ladder to the fifth floor wasn't an option.

The doorman ran alongside me, opened the entrance when we reached it, and pointed me toward the stairs. The visibility on the ground level was fine, and smoke hadn't entered the inside of the stairwell, either. I took each flight as quickly as I could. Four sets of stairs with seventy-five pounds of gear was only possible at break-neck speed when adrenaline was involved. I prayed to God there was only one person involved. I'd never get more than that out on my own, and Lord help me if there were an adult and a child.

Heavy footfalls of another man echoed behind me, but I didn't turn or wait to see who it was. I breathed heavily through the mask as I found my way to the penthouse. Smoke billowed under the door, tickling the carpet with embers. Each crackle sparked confetti flames that danced at my feet.

"Fire department!" I could feel the heat from the other side, and I wondered if the entire apartment was engulfed; hopefully, whoever was inside had found a pocket of air or opened a window.

The knob didn't budge when I tried to turn it, no one answered when I called out again, and right as Nick sidled up next to me, I slammed my Halligan tool into the frame and kicked down the door. Glass blew out from somewhere inside, and I was lucky I hadn't been caught in a backdraft.

A sea of fire rolled in through the entrance I'd just busted through, and the waves came in like a tsunami. There was no telling what had started the blaze, but there wouldn't be anything left by the time we got it put out.

Thick, black smoke hung in the air, and flares slid up the walls surrounding us. "Hello?" The living room appeared to be empty, but as I moved farther back with Nick at my heels, more men came at our rear, fanning out to check the perimeter.

Water started to pour in through the broken windows, and smoke chased freedom into the night air. The only light in the penthouse came from the inferno surrounding me. Sweat trickled down my neck and back, and the heat became oppressive. I refused to give up until I found the person I'd seen in the window. With each step I took, the fire followed me deeper into the apartment.

I'd nearly reached the end of the hall and had come up empty-handed. There was no way out. Whoever I'd seen was still in here, hiding, and it was unlikely he or she could hear me call out over the roar of the sirens and the fire. The oxygen pumped into my mask, and the hollow echo of my breathing made it difficult for me to differentiate the sounds. But flames and smoke weren't unique, they had patterns and moved the same way regardless of where they burned. One thing they never did was sit still.

Even without much visibility, there was no doubt the lump near the window was a human being. And if my memory served me, it was the same window I'd seen a figure in. In seconds, I'd scooped her into my arms. Her long hair covered her face and arms, and somehow, her robe had stayed wrapped around her when I'd lifted her from the floor.

There wasn't time for any type of medical intervention, and the best I'd be able to do was get her oxygen once I'd gotten on the other side of this blaze. Nick was still at my back, but he turned to lead us out as soon as I had her secure in my embrace.

"Come on lady, don't die on me." I talked to myself as much as I did to her. I didn't know if she could hear me or not. All I knew was if it were me, I'd want to know someone was with me. "Hang in there." *Fuck.*

Her head had lulled to the side over my forearm, lifeless.

"We're losing her, Nick. Radio EMT." I wasn't a doctor, but I didn't need an M.D. to realize she was in trouble. I had no idea how long the fire burned before someone had notified the department, nor did I have a clue when she'd run out of fresh air. She was covered in ash, and her robe was filthy.

I cradled her against my chest as I followed Nick out of the flames and down the stairwell. My thighs ached, and my lungs burned. "We're almost there," I shouted through my mask, hoping she could hear me.

As the air cleared and we hit the ground floor, her eyes flittered. Disoriented and scared, she pushed against my mask and struggled to get away from me. The emergency lights flickered in the halls, and something crashed above us. The woman rolled into my embrace and clung to my neck.

"It's okay. I'm gonna get you out of here." I doubted my assurances did much for her, but I did my best to keep her calm until I got her to the paramedics just outside the building entrance.

When the EMTs tried to take her, she almost refused to let me go. Once they'd wrangled her from my arms, she was swept away on a gurney in a sea of medical personnel.

I didn't get a chance to look at her, so I didn't know if she had any other injuries. My mask was fogged up, and I had to let the EMTs do their job. I'd get reamed for putting myself in jeopardy before this was all over, but right now, my guys were struggling to contain the blaze. My heart still raced, and my blood pumped through my veins vigorously. The other men had cleared the floor and exited shortly after me. Once the final man hit the lawn, I slumped against the engine and yanked off my mask and dumped my gear.

A couple of hard-fought hours later, four engines had managed to stop the blaze, but the entire building was lost. The people who'd stood on the grass when we had arrived were long since gone, and all but one of the ambulances had pulled off. We were the last of the last there, which wasn't unusual. When I'd finished packing our rig, I rounded the truck to see the woman I'd pulled from the building, staring at the charred wreckage—alone.

The fact that she was standing was a good sign. Her being alone was not. This shit was scary. It was raw and real. In the blink of an eye, people lost their homes—everything they owned—and others lost their lives.

I found the EMT by the driver's door of the ambulance. "She okay?"

"Yeah, we're going to let her go." The paramedic's shoulders dropped. She'd been here as long as we had. "She refused medical treatment, and we can't force it on her. But I think she's making a mistake." The lady shook her head and closed the back of the ambulance before giving a nod to her partner.

I hadn't taken my eyes off the woman, but she hadn't turned. She just stared at what was left of her home with her arms wrapped around her midsection, hugging herself. An officer approached her to make his report, and I was going to let it go at that. Until the woman turned to the policeman at her side.

Brayleigh.

Uncertain who to give her attention to, her eyes went wide—big and brown, shocked—and darted between the officer and me. Her lips parted, and her hands flew in front of her face as she gasped, "Oh, no..." She didn't keep her gorgeous features hidden; instead, Brayleigh combed her fingers through her messy hair.

I couldn't tell if it was embarrassment, shame, or some other emotion that had her flustered, but the officer nodded and gave us a minute alone.

"Yeah, I could say the same thing. You start fires in your free time?" I moved closer and tried to comfort her with humor and a smile.

She gazed up at me when I stopped in front of her. A swarm of emotion swirled in her irises. "You fight fires in yours?"

I cleared my throat. "Something like that."

"You should go to the hospital. Get checked out. Smoke inhalation is no joke, Brayleigh."

This wasn't my idea of fate or serendipity, but I didn't have a clue what else to do with her in front of me. I never thought I'd see her again much less on a call. Yet, here she was, homeless, and I'd been the one to pull her from the wreckage.

"I'm fine." She swallowed hard and squeezed herself as a chilly wind bustled through.

"Carter, you with us?" Nick hollered from across the lawn.

I turned and held up my finger to get him to give me a minute. They were still loading, but time wasn't on my side...just coincidence.

"Don't be silly. Why wouldn't you want to make sure nothing's wrong?"

She shook her head and glanced back at the building. "It's just...I was half asleep." Brayleigh was either confused or in shock. "They checked me out. I'm okay." Clearly, she hadn't seen me talking to the EMT. She touched her neck with her delicate fingers, and I had to stop myself from remembering what they'd looked like wrapped around my cock. "My throat just hurts. If I feel worse, I'll go to the emergency room." Her eyes had gone vacant, but I wasn't sure why. She was definitely coherent, not rambling—just...lost.

I took her hand in mine, and she looked down at our fingers curled together and then back into my eyes. "You sure?"

Her soft cheekbones were flushed pink and dusted with ash, and her full lips were chapped from the heat. The whites of her eyes were tinted red, and I'd guess they burned like hell from the smoke. But I'd seen far worse outcomes. With a shower and a good night's sleep, she'd *look* good as new. Mentally, that might take a while.

"Yeah, Carter. I'm sure."

I squeezed her hand and then let it go. She wrapped her arm around herself again and stared off into the night. I didn't have long to hang around, and the officer still waited off to the side to take her statement.

"Where are you going to go?" I tilted my head toward what remained of her building. "The fire marshal and police have to check your place out for insurance, but it's not safe for you to go up there, anyhow."

Brayleigh was far too calm for what she'd just gone through. At the very least, I expected her to freak out about having lost her things and her home. But she just stood there, stoically. "Um...maybe a hotel? I don't know."

I glanced at the clock, it was almost three in the morning, and I seriously doubted she had her car keys in the pocket of her robe much less a credit card. "Why don't you come to my place? I'd feel better knowing you weren't alone." I didn't typically give a rip if a woman was alone or not, but I couldn't fight the universe, and Mother Nature had dropped me at her door.

"I don't want to impose. You've already done enough." Her cheeks flushed again. Innocence looked good on her. "Saving my life and all." She swallowed back her embarrassment.

This always made shit awkward. People stamped you with a status just for doing your job. And a hero, I was not.

"Yeah, but...I'm a little worried about you." I touched her elbow and hoped she saw the sincerity in my eyes because that was as close to an admission of wanting to see a woman again as I could get. "I'm sure I've got something you can wear until you get in touch with your friends."

Brayleigh didn't seem sold on the idea, and Nick kept calling my name. I didn't have a lot of time to convince her.

"Look, I can give you the key and get an officer to drop you off. My shift doesn't end until seven, so I won't even be there. You can shower, rummage through my drawers for a shirt and shorts, and call your friends at a decent hour. Hell, you might even take a nap." I was quite certain the last one wouldn't happen, but I wasn't opposed to coming home to a beautiful woman in my bed just this once. I made my last plea. "The last place you want to be after something like this is a hotel."

Her sight dropped to my feet, and she nodded hesitantly. When she looked back up, I saw the reluctance written all over her face. There was a part of her that wanted to say yes, and another that needed to say no. Thank fuck the yes won out. "I guess that would be okay. Thank you."

I told her where the spare key to my house was and told her to make herself at home. I didn't know what force had brought us back together, but I had a hard time blocking out the nagging voice that told me not to push her away.

Chapter Seven

I watched Carter as he joined his friends and the officer joined me. I had no idea what I was thinking going to his house, but when he'd squeezed my hand and released me, I'd felt a loss I didn't care to identify. And I certainly didn't reach out for him. Then when he'd left and I still stared at the spot I'd last seen him, I wondered if I'd fallen for the man who'd saved me. Maybe my feelings had been amplified in some mental disorder when he'd carried me out of a burning building. Whether the feelings were legitimate or imagined, they still existed, and they twisted my stomach into knots. Or maybe that was the smoke inhalation making me sick.

I wanted nothing more than to reach out to my friends, but I couldn't bring myself to call anyone at three o'clock in the morning. Gabby worked weird shifts at the hospital, and I sure wasn't going to stay at her place alone with James. And Riley's apartment was the size of a shoebox which wouldn't be so bad except she was a slob. Even if I didn't have another option, Riley's wasn't a choice. It was way too late to call my friends to ask for a place to stay just because I'd burned mine down. That story could wait until daylight.

As mindboggling as this whole incident had been, I couldn't stop the obsessive thoughts that ran through my head. This was all about to get really messy, between insurance companies and my father finding out that I'd managed to knock over a candle in my sleep, I needed some stress relief sooner rather than later, and Carter could provide just that. I didn't know what it said about me that I had sex on my mind and an officer in my face with a building full of ash behind me.

I managed to keep from losing my mind while the officer got my statement regarding what happened, and I didn't miss the smirk or the shake of his head. He didn't bother to hide that he knew who I was or his feelings about my part in multiple families currently being without a place to stay. I bit my tongue long enough to get the case number for the insurance company, but since I wasn't the owner of the building, they would be reaching out to him as well.

My dad would have a field day with this. Once he knew I was okay, he'd lay into me about destroying a building. Then I'd get a lecture about why I insisted on living alone and not in New York. It would spiral into an argument about why I wanted independence, which he would claim I didn't really have since I lived off his name. That wasn't exactly true, but he did manage my finances and my meager income. I groaned, dreading it all.

As the guy finished with me, another officer emerged from the building with what appeared to be my purse. "Is this yours?" She held it out as an offering. "That was the only thing I saw inside that was salvageable." Her grim smile gave me more hope than she could have imagined. "Oh, and I found this." The policewoman pulled my cell from her breast pocket.

I didn't have a clue how she'd located either. I clutched the bag to my chest, thankful I now had my cell phone, keys, wallet, and my emergency panties. The Louis Viton was singed and pretty dingy, but my stuff inside appeared fine. "Thank you."

She rubbed my upper arm. "Hang on. Let me see if I've got some sweats in the patrol car. They won't be much, but it's better than roaming around in a robe." She didn't comment on the condition of the soot-covered garment, which I appreciated.

A few moments later, she returned with a grey hoodie and pants that were more comfortable than I'd thought they'd be when I slid them up my legs. I signed the paperwork, and the officer let me go.

It was surreal walking away from a fire I'd started, and I didn't know why I felt like I was walking into another one.

I PARKED IN HIS DRIVEWAY AND WENT through the front door like I lived there. It was weird how familiar it all felt and how oddly comforting it was to be in a place that seemed normal. Albeit, I didn't remember a lot about the place beside Carter's bed, and I ended up circling twice before deciding I'd stick to what I knew—Carter's room. The sheets were different, but his room was the same. Everything was in order, nothing out of place. *I* wasn't even that neat, and I was rather obsessive about cleanliness. It even smelled like him, that warm piney scent.

The sweats weren't as comfortable as they'd been when I first put them on, although that probably had more to do with the soot and smoke that now permeated the air around me. When I realized that stench was me, I decided it was not only time to change, but I also needed to trash the clothing outside when I was done.

In the master bathroom, I stripped off my clothes and opened the glass door. The hot water came through quickly, and I stepped under the spray. A swirl of grey trailed down my legs and onto the bright-white tile at my feet. I waited until the water ran clear before I started to wash my hair and body. I wasn't keen on smelling like men's body wash, but when

Carter's scent filled the large shower, I felt like I was home.

Once the water finally ran cold, I gave up and got out. His towels were plush and large enough to use at the beach. I wrapped myself in one and my hair in another. I hated to snoop, but I opened the cabinets and drawers looking for lotion. It was amazing what I realized I no longer had now that I'd lost everything. And apparently, Carter didn't have lotion, either. I kept telling myself it wasn't snooping if he'd told me to make myself at home, and he hadn't indicated where I'd find a T-shirt or shorts. Thankfully, I found both in the first two drawers I opened.

I may look like a drowned rat without a round brush or a hair dryer or a flat iron, but I was safe and clean. His heather-grey shirt read fire department and had the emblem emblazoned on the back. It also swallowed me whole. The boxers wouldn't stay up, so I opted to go without. There wasn't a single inch of me that Carter hadn't seen, so sitting around in my panties and his shirt shouldn't be an issue.

I finally found myself on his couch, wrapped in a fleece blanket, and once I'd figured out how to work his remote, I landed on a station playing old sitcoms. I'd fooled myself into thinking I'd had a full night's sleep. My body and mind were exhausted, and it took no time for my lids to droop. But before I allowed myself to sleep, I checked to make sure nothing could start a fire.

THE FRONT DOOR SLAMMED, STARTLING ME from my nap. I was still groggy when my lids parted, and it took me a moment to realize where I was. I rubbed my eyes with the heel of my hand and looked around. Carter hadn't come around the corner, and I hoped he didn't have a roommate that I wasn't aware of.

I stumbled over my words when he finally leaned his head around the corner. "Oh, hi. I was, um, watching television. I hope you don't mind." I craned my neck to stare at him and felt the heat rise from my throat up to my cheeks where it settled. Without make-up on, I was quite certain my face was crimson red.

Somehow, Carter looked sexier in jeans and a navy hoodie than he had that night at the club. And when that smirk ticked up his lip, I wished I hadn't bothered with his shirt.

"Not at all. Did you get some sleep?

The sun shined through the window behind him as he approached, and I realized I'd slept longer than intended. "I did. Thanks for letting me crash while you were gone." I tried to calm my wildly curly hair each time I saw him glance up at it.

He pointed at the mess on top of my head. "That's cute. You should wear it curly."

I groaned. It was not cute. It was a bird's nest, and any hope for a repeat of that night at Right Nine went out the window.

But even after I'd shown my disapproval and disagreement, Carter hadn't looked away. There was a hint of something soft that lingered in his gaze, although I didn't have a clue what it was. He cleared his throat. "It was a pretty intense night. I had another call after yours, and I'm beat." Carter paused like he expected me to speak, but I stayed quiet. "I'm going to go shower. You good for a bit?"

"Yeah, sure. Take your time." What the hell was I thinking? It was his damn house. I didn't need to tell him what to do or how to do it. I sucked at this.

He walked off to his bedroom, and I collapsed back onto the couch with an audible sigh. Every inch of me craved Carter at a time that couldn't be more inappropriate, yet all I wanted to do was join him and let him have his way with me. Carter could not only make me forget my name, but he could drown out the memories of what had taken place a few hours earlier.

Instead of thinking about the god of fire being wet and naked in the other room, I took the time to make some calls and start to get my life in order. The first call I had to make was to my insurance company to give them the case number for my personal belongings. Then I called my dad, waiting for the lecture to come and to have to sit through it. He'd proven me right in the lecture, but once he'd learned everyone was all right, he'd let it drop. Clearly, he was off his game. It was the perfect chance for him to force me back to New York where he could hover and try to force me into some arranged marriage, but not a word was said.

The insurance company called me back

right as I hung up with my dad to tell me which hotel they had made arrangements with for my undetermined length of stay. It would be several weeks before I'd see a check, so I'd have to use my credit card to go shopping or borrow clothes from Riley. My shoulders slumped when I realized I'd have to repeat this story at least two more times to Gabby and Riley. I glanced at the clock and convinced myself it was too early to call either friend, and there would be time for that later. I couldn't stay on a stranger's couch forever, and I needed to get myself together and get going.

"You hungry?" His voice bellowed into the living room, and I jumped as he walked past me.

My mouth watered at the sight of that eight pack and the track pants that rode low on his trim hips. I was hungry all right, but not for food. "No, thanks. I'm okay." I bit my lip and stood, following him into the kitchen. "How was the rest of work?" I asked him casually as if we were a thing and did this regularly.

He opened his fridge and smirked at me over the door. "Long. We had another call that lasted a couple hours." Carter snatched a bottle of water, removed the cap, and drank nearly half of it while standing in the cool air of the opened door. No one should look that edible downing a beverage.

"Is it always this fast-paced?" I leaned my hip against the counter, crossing my arms over my chest.

He stopped drinking, and his eyes did that thing where they assessed every inch of my body as if they were his hands. The gleam told me that he liked what he saw, or maybe he remembered—like I did—what lay underneath. "Not really. Some days are better than others. But it's hard to decide if not having any calls is better than successfully responding to them. There's something satisfying about putting out fires without anyone dying, including myself." He chuckled, but I didn't get the impression that he laughed because he thought it was funny, more like it was ironic.

I didn't know where to go from here. I didn't do relationships or repeats. Once on that crazy train had been enough for me, and I'd never boarded again. Yet even in the silence, there was nothing awkward.

I filled him in on what little information I

had about the insurance company, leaving out the part about my wealthy father taking care of the brunt of it. That was a secret I kept guarded when I could. It changed people's perception of me almost instantly, and it was obvious Carter was oblivious to who I was or that I came from society. He was absolutely the type to be turned off by wealth, and I wasn't quite ready to divulge that truth if I didn't have to.

"Thanks again for letting me hang out until the sun came up. I really appreciate it."

I wanted to ask if it meant anything, or if he'd just done a good deed. I wanted to ask if he wanted a repeat as desperately as I did. I wanted to ask him to throw me over his shoulder and have his way with me. But I didn't. I didn't do *any* of that. I was too focused on the way he moved as he approached me.

My eyes held his until he was less than an inch away. I could have licked his lips; we stood so close. My knees went weak, and I wondered if he felt that same pull, that same electricity, the same...something that kept me on edge and turned on.

"I told you, Brayleigh, it wasn't a problem." My name sounded like a fine wine when it passed his lips, and his pupils constricted and returned to their normal size when he inhaled what could only have been my scent.

"Well, I just—" I didn't even remember what I was going to say before his lips descended upon mine.

The kiss was like a thousand pieces coming together. The stress of the night, the security of his arms, the anticipation of seeing him here. It all came crashing down onto my mouth in an epic crescendo. Carter kissed me roughly, and I responded, opening my lips to his as our tongues collided. Our bodies met, pressing against each other in a perfect fit, my breasts pillowing against his hard chest as he held me close. In seconds, his hands were everywhere, but once they'd found the hem of my shirt, Carter grasped my ass. With nothing but thin panties on underneath, the heat of his skin on mine made my core swell and my pussy wet.

Carter growled when he shifted my weight onto his thigh and ground my sensitive nub onto the hard muscle of his leg. My moan was shameless and relentless, begging for more than he'd given.

My fingers fisted into his soft hair, and I

angled my head to deepen the kiss. I couldn't get enough of the pleasure he offered. The entire experience was surreal, but it was, and it felt so...*right*.

The two of us melded together in harmony, and I wondered where he'd been all this time and if I'd get to keep him. But that was a question I'd never ask, so instead, I just kissed him like the ship was going down. I'd hold on until the very last minute, but there was no way in hell, I'd sink with the boat.

"Shit, Brayleigh, you're fucking irresistible." He spoke breathlessly against my lips before trailing kisses down my neck, finding that place that made me mewl.

I dropped my head and slumped against the counter when his hand slid up between my legs, grazing my thigh before reaching my clit. My pussy throbbed for him, an ache that only Carter had ever created and only he could satisfy. In seconds, he had my panties down my legs and on the floor and had slid two, thick fingers inside me, curling up to tease my G-spot.

"Carter..." I could barely speak, much less coherently. "Don't stop." I gasped.

He fingered me like none other ever had, actually hitting all my pleasure spots. And when his palm pressed onto my tiny bundle of nerves while his fingers fucked me, I nearly came undone in his kitchen. My vision blurred until I snapped my eyes shut entirely, desperate to stave off the pending orgasm.

Carter knew exactly what he was doing, teasing me with his hands and torturing me with his cock. He pressed his hard length against my thigh, rubbing. I'd gone from gripping the counter like it was a lifeline to dragging my hands down the rock-hard planes of his chest until my fingers dipped into the waistband of his pants. His skin was smooth and warm and soft, and his cock was mighty and thick.

Carter groaned against my ear when my hand circled his shaft, and he nipped at my lip as I started to pump his engorged dick. I dragged the moisture from his tip with my thumb, sliding it down as I went. The faster he worked me, the less I did him. I couldn't focus when my insides began to pulse, and once I'd gone over the edge, I wasn't able to even hang on. My body coiled tight, erupted, and then collapsed. But Carter never let up.

"Holy shit, Carter..." I bit my lip, panting and tried to catch my breath.

He left me a ravaged mess on the counter as he took off my shirt, exposing my body to his. The cold air hit my nipples, hardening them with a sudden temperature change and undeniable arousal.

"Damn." His bright blue eyes roamed my body as he breathed heavily.

Realizing I caused his chest to expand and contract like he couldn't get enough air made my heart swell. There was something about knowing I'd garnered that reaction—the flexed muscles and flushed skin—that made him the sexiest man alive. The look was gone as fast as it came, and I'd almost missed it when he hitched me over his shoulder. With a slap on the ass, he carried me off to the bedroom.

In less than ten steps, he'd made it down the hall and tossed me onto the mattress. One bounce was all he allowed me before he climbed on top, taking my lips with his. It was as passionate as it was desperate.

I nearly cried out when Carter pushed

himself off the bed to grab a condom from the drawer. But once he'd shed his pants, he was back, kneeling between my thighs. I watched with rapt attention as he slid the latex over his swollen head and then rolled it down his thick shaft. He was big, and he knew it. Carter did not, however, rely on his size to impress the ladies—he worked what God had given him.

My knees butterflied to welcome him, and he grabbed the backs of my thighs. Our eyes met—and locked—when he slid his dick inside of me, slowly, inch by glorious inch until he'd reached the hilt. Carter couldn't go any deeper.

"Oh, God..." I moaned as he started to move, falling into a rhythm.

He grunted with each thrust, and the headboard rattled with his motion. My breast swayed with the rough way he took me, but all I could do was hold on. I clenched the sheets and opened as wide as I could for him. My body climbed higher by the second, nearing that peak faster than I'd believed possible. He knew exactly where to touch me, and how long he wanted to draw it out. It was like I couldn't come until he wanted me to, and when he did, God, did I come.

I saw so many stars, I might as well have been in a different galaxy. The milky way had nothing on Carter.

"Fuck," he cursed before he lost control. Then in seconds, he stilled inside of me, digging his fingers into my thighs as he came. His abs tensed, the tendons in his neck corded, and he roared like the mightiest lion in the pride. And then his heat simmered inside me as it filled me from the inside out.

Carter moved my legs, laying against my body when he took my lips. I rolled us onto our sides and kept kissing him. That connection was as good as the sex, although I didn't know why. I'd never kissed for emotion, just stimulation, but whatever Carter drew out of me, I craved more.

His hands explored my body, grasping my ass, my breasts. He just kept doing it all on repeat until he tossed the condom, ready to start again.

Chapter Eight

I'd been wrong before when I'd just imagined that Brayleigh was the best I'd ever had. It wasn't just a memory fucking with my head. She truly was in a league all her own, and I couldn't get enough of her. Which freaked me the fuck out. I tried to convince myself it was because I had a connection to her prior to the fire, then rescuing her put her in some class that tied her to me like I was designed to protect her. But I was designed to protect anyone who needed me, not just her. Yet no matter how hard I tried to tell myself there was an alternate reason for the way my heart skipped when she entered the room, or my chest expanded when she smiled, none of me believed that shit. The only explanation was that she *was* different.

That, however, changed nothing. No relationships. No commitments. No strings. It was easier for everyone that way. And not even her long hair covering my chest, or the feel of her breathing in my arms, or the way she moaned my name when I made her come would change that.

Brayleigh pushed herself off my chest and sat up in bed. "I shouldn't sleep all day. It will mess up my schedule." Her eyes were still a tad bloodshot, but overall, she'd handled the ordeal far better than anyone I'd ever seen. She held the sheet to her chest and let out a long sigh, but it wasn't frustration. It resembled contentment.

Despite how that sound worried me, I still allowed my eyes to rove over her back and down her spine to the slope of her ass. Brayleigh had a fantastic body with full hips and a thick butt. But falling for the way she looked wouldn't get either of us anywhere. And the best thing I could do was let her—and the phenomenal sex—go. The longer it went on, the more hurt she'd be, and I didn't want to do that to her.

"Did you get everything in order with the insurance company?" I realized as soon as the question left my mouth how it had sounded, and the look she gave me over her bare shoulder confirmed it.

The hurt I didn't want to see lingered just behind her eyes. It was in the hooded way she regarded me. And it was most certainly in the pitiful excuse she offered up as humor in response. "Is that your way of politely kicking me out?" Her laugh fell short, and I felt like an ass.

I sat up and cleared my throat. "No. It's not." I swallowed, trying to figure out whether I meant that or not.

Her shoulders slumped, and the sheet fell from her chest, exposing her pert tits and flat stomach when she scooted off the mattress. She grabbed my shirt off the floor and pulled it over her head. I waited for her to say something, but Brayleigh stood at the foot of the bed, staring down at me.

"I'm just going to take a shower if that's

okay?" She bit her lip, and uncertainty lined her brow. This was a girl who was used to getting what she wanted when she wanted it. People didn't tell her no, much less men.

I nodded. "Yeah, for sure."

I mentally cursed myself as she walked off and then shut the door. This was why I didn't do repeats. Women got attached, and once that happened, I'd be the asshole who ended things. And even worse with Brayleigh, I'd be the cocksucker who fucked her, dragged her out of a blazing inferno less than twenty-four hours ago, opened my home, and then kicked her out. I got whiplash contemplating the emotional jerkoff just thinking about it.

As much as I hated to hurt her or make things worse for her than they already were, I was a dead end. She'd be better off to find that out now, and I had to set her straight before it was too late...without being rude.

I listened for the shower to stop running, then I got up and got dressed in jeans and a T-shirt. Working at the station could be grueling. Twenty-four on shift meant forty-eight off, but those twenty-four could be tough. I usually used my first day off to do a whole lot of nothing other than ordering takeout and watching any game I could find on TV.

I flopped onto the couch after I'd ordered lunch and flipped through the stations until I'd settled on basketball. The pillows already smelled like her which was odd because she'd used my shampoo and soap to shower. Yet her scent was everywhere, and now, I didn't want to imagine what it would be like without it. It would fade quickly, but her memory wouldn't. It was subtle, but it caught my attention just the same.

It wasn't fair to have to do this to her. I didn't even know her. She didn't know me. But I couldn't deny that there was a bond between us that had been there before I'd pulled her out of that building, and it had only gotten stronger once I'd realize it was her standing on the grass. And another sexual encounter hadn't dusted off any of the emotional overload, either. Brayleigh would be the distraction that would wind up getting me killed or worse, someone else.

Brayleigh wandered in from down the hall. My sweats swallowed her completely, but it was the sheepish look on her face that I found

so adorable. A smile rose on my lips, and I realized it wasn't the way her nipples peaked the
shirt. It was just Brayleigh. Seeing her.

"I borrowed a shirt." She held it out to the
side as if I hadn't recognized it. "I hope you
don't mind." She chewed the inside of her
cheek, causing her lips to purse and my mind to
race with thoughts of where those lips had been
not all that long ago.

"Nah. Wanna sit?" I patted the cushion at
my side.

Her eyes widened a bit, and her brow
arched in question, but she didn't ask anything.
Instead, she plopped down next to me. Her hair
was still damp and incredibly curly. I wondered
how my shampoo smelled so different on her.
In seconds, I was mentally slapping myself out
of the web she'd weaved with her natural
beauty and charm. Brayleigh was a knockout
dressed up, but she was simply stunning kicked
back, sans makeup, wearing my clothes.

"Who's playing?" She stared at the screen.

I never understood why chicks did that.
There was no need to pretend they were interested in sports just because a guy was. "Celtics
and the Knicks."

I stared at her in wonder, when she rattled off stats for both teams and folded her legs beneath her. "You're a basketball fan?"

Brayleigh shrugged. "My dad was pretty into it when I was growing up. It just stuck with me."

That only amped up the level of interest that I needed to be squashing. I couldn't spend any more time getting to know her. Even if she didn't get attached, I could end up falling for a girl who looked like Brayleigh and could actually discuss players in the NBA. Every detail I learned made her spell more potent. "I ordered Chinese."

"It's barely eleven."

And I'd spent several hours working up an appetite with the brunette at my side. "Yeah, my days run a bit differently than most people's." Being around her was effortless when I just let go. Without thought, I swung my arm over her shoulders.

Brayleigh stiffened a bit, glanced up at me, and then relaxed into my embrace. Easy was dangerous. This would be catastrophic.

"How did you get used to it?"

I turned down the television, but her eyes didn't leave the game. "The schedule?"

She nodded, and I realized I wanted to talk to her. I'd never had the urge to open up to a chick, much less share anything with one about work or my life. "I don't know. I've been doing it for so long that I don't really think about it anymore. The hardest part are the shifts where we get call after call and never have any downtime. But that happens less often than you'd think." I shrugged, drawing her in closer. "It's just one of those jobs you have to be made for. No one wakes up one day and decides to be a firefighter. You're either born wanting to do it, or you don't make it." *Or you die because you fuck up when your heart's not in it.*

The delivery guy saved me from any further intimate interaction, casual or otherwise. It was funny how I didn't mind getting naked, it was the bearing my soul that I couldn't handle. We could fuck all day if that kept her happy.

I got up to answer the door and struck up a conversation with the regular delivery driver. But just like everything else, even my rituals— the ones I did alone—seemed normal with

Brayleigh at my side. I typically ate by myself, but if I had company, it was always one of the guys.

Brayleigh tapped her fingers, and I could tell she was restless. "I'm going to update my friends." It was abrupt, but I just figured she'd needed to move.

I cleaned up what little mess there was and went back to my spot on the couch. Nick and Brian had both sent me messages. Nick was pissed. I'd left him at the station, and he'd had to walk home after a long shift, and Brian wanted us to all get together for dinner tonight.

I brushed off Nick with a half-assed apology and told Brian it would depend on how I felt, which was partially true. I didn't know how to get out without asking her to join me, but introducing her to my friends, taking her to dinner at a buddy's house—nope. That was a line I wouldn't cross; I didn't care how much she liked basketball. It implied that something could take place, a commitment that couldn't happen. When I came home, it had to be alone. Because one night was temporary, two were comfortable, and three, I didn't want to think about.

The only way to break free from this was short and sweet. I walked back into the living room and swallowed my conscience. "Hey, I have plans later. I'm not racing you out or anything, but I didn't want to leave you here alone, either. Any idea how long you might need to hang out?" I was the biggest fucking dick that ever walked the planet. I wouldn't have to worry about whether or not she had feelings for me after that proclamation. I might as well just have opened the door and told her to have a nice life.

She held her cell in her hand as she sat on the couch. "Oh God, I'm sorry. I didn't mean to get in the way." Brayleigh stood quickly, and it was obvious she forced the smile that resided on her lips. "I'm sure the insurance company has everything in place at the hotel. I'll get out of your hair." I'd never heard her speak with so much nonchalance, and I realized she tried to keep the hurt and rejection from her tone.

"I don't want to rush you out of here or anything. I just um...." I scratched at the back of my head like the answer was there, all while giving her a placid look.

She swallowed, but it got stuck in her

throat, and a frown broke through before she could mask it. "No, no. I get it." Brayleigh rolled her ankle and bit her lip. "I'm so sorry. I didn't mean to intrude. Let me just get my purse, and I'll get going." She turned to walk toward my bedroom and stopped. Her chin dropped to her chest, and her voice cracked when she spoke. "Can I borrow the clothes I have on until Riley brings me some things to the hotel?"

I stood there like a jackass, but I didn't comfort her or apologize. I didn't run to her and tell her why I had to make her go. "Yeah, of course." They were just sweats, and I could almost guarantee after the way I'd just talked to this girl, she'd never show her face here again to give them back.

I wish relationships weren't so tricky. That I could just see where this went without trying to sabotage it, but I'd made up my mind for a reason. And that decision was made a long time ago, a long time before Brayleigh.

"Brayleigh, look, I didn't mean to—" I walked into my room where she had grabbed her purse that looked more like melted plastic. I was an insensitive jackass. The woman had nothing, and I couldn't even manage to be a friend.

She held up her hand. "It's fine, Carter." Her eyes were cold, and her voice was hollow. "Clearly, I misread the signals. It seemed like more than just sex. Like there was possibly something there." She squared her shoulders and straightened her spine, and I realized she'd put up a wall, and that wall would be impenetrable once she'd put the final brick in it. "I don't want to walk out that door without asking, without getting the truth."

Her lip quivered, and she stood there, waiting. That was the moment I was supposed to change her mind and actually tell her the truth. Now was the time I should admit she wasn't crazy, that I'd felt that electricity, the chemistry, the connection. There *was* something there.

But I didn't do that. Instead, I helped her finish building that wall to keep out men like me. "The truth is that I just wanted to help. The sex was great, the fire was unfortunate, but at the end of the day...it was just sex." I held her eyes when I said the next two words—the only two that held any truth. "I'm sorry." I released a heavy sigh and knew I'd let something else go with it.

She stared back at me, sullen, but her expression never faltered, and she never shed a tear. I forced myself to ignore the stabbing pang in my chest and the emptiness that followed. I already felt like an idiot, and she hadn't even left yet.

She put her bag over her shoulder, and with the grace and dignity of a well-bred woman, she held her head high. "Don't be sorry, Carter. I asked for the truth." Brayleigh stopped in front of me, looking up into my eyes.

Another golden opportunity. She hadn't left—yet. I could stop her from walking out my door and out of my life. All it would take was one word.

Brayleigh placed her palm on my chest. "Thanks for your help, Carter." And she strolled out the door without so much as a glance back.

I stared across the table at Brian and Nick. Both of my asshole friends had taken turns stabbing me with insults and scolding my decision to ask Brayleigh to leave. I didn't need these two jackasses confirming how stupid I was or making me feel worse, both of which they did with vigor.

I'd had all I could stand when I finally snapped. "Okay, enough. I was only doing the right thing."

"Since when is letting a hot girl that you clearly dig leave your house the right thing?" Nick laughed.

I shook my head. "It wasn't about that. I just didn't want her to get attached."

Brian stared at me with one brow cocked in disbelief. "You didn't want *her* to get attached, or you were freaked because you saw yourself getting attached?"

Explaining myself to these two was pointless. "It was supposed to be one night. You both know that. You were there. You saw her. We all agreed, hit and quit it." I darted my focus between the two, hoping one of them would agree. "She was never supposed to be a keeper. Come on!"

Neither one gave in, and I gave up. I nursed my beer while Brian did the dishes and Erika left without getting involved in the conversation. *Coward.* She was the only one on my side, and she'd left me to the wolves.

"Whether it was supposed to be one night or not, you not only saw her again, you saved her life. And then like a total fucking dickwad, you invited her to your house after she lost everything. You freaked because she was there, and now you're freaked because she won't be back." Brian shook his head. "Carter, man, you've been single for a really long time—"

"Exactly. That's why I don't know how to do this."

Nick clapped my shoulder. "Well, I can assure you that kicking her out was not the right move."

"I didn't kick her out, Nick." I huffed and had to count to five to keep from punching him. "I'm not a total Neanderthal, you goon." I shoved my friend, nearly knocking him off the stool next to me.

Nick managed to keep his balance without hitting the floor. "Sounded like it to me. Do you know where she is staying?"

I shrugged. She'd left two days ago, and I only knew where she was staying because she mailed back my clothes in a box with the hotel's return address. I'd been shocked when I opened the package. She'd told me she'd return them, but I'd assumed she'd do what all women did...use it as an excuse to see me again. Not Brayleigh—she didn't want any kind of reminder of me at all. That wall she'd built standing in my house had been formed on a solid foundation.

But I didn't blame her. I'd done everything I could to eradicate her scent from my house, and when that damn box showed up, the second I opened it, the floral smell I loved so much—the one from the night we'd met— wafted into my house, and it hadn't left. It haunted me, fucked with me.

"Yeah, I've got the address." I ran my hand through my hair and stared at Nick. "But I doubt she wants to see me."

"Not unless you're apologizing. I've never met this girl, but since we've never spoken at length about any other female in your life, I have to assume this one's special." Then Nick ruined a perfectly poetic statement by belching and chugging more beer.

I wasn't sure which of the three of us was

more lost, but I thought maybe it was Nick. I laughed and shook my head. I didn't know if I could fix this, and I was certain even if I managed to that I'd fuck it up a hundred more times along the way. But one thing was for sure. I had to try.

I just hoped it wasn't too late.

Chapter Nine

My heart had raced as I tried casually exiting Carter's house. And even days later, every time I thought about it, I got upset. It had taken everything in me to act unaffected, to stay calm, not to show emotion as he rejected me. None of it made any sense. There was no way he hadn't felt what I had; it was too electric, too charged. The chemistry between us was unbelievable, yet he'd let me walk away without so much as an ounce of hesitation. Each kiss had been real, wrought with emotion. When he'd been inside of me, it was more than just fucking. I hadn't misread *all* of that.

Clearly, my mind had tricked my heart into

believing something that didn't exist after he'd saved my life. What was extraordinary to me was normal for Carter. It was just his job. It was not his job, however, to invite me to his house or fuck me seven ways from Sunday. Coupled with the night's events, those two things were definitely out of the ordinary. Carter hadn't offered because he'd had to. I had options. I could have stayed at a hotel with no trouble, but he'd wanted me there.

I'd racked my brain and nearly driven myself insane thinking about where things had jumped the track. My friends had deftly reminded me at every turn that I hadn't needed to be at a stranger's house or a hotel after something as catastrophic as losing my home, but I'd held my ground to try to un-muddle my life. After two hours of self-imposed isolation, I invited Gabby and Riley to the hotel for some much-needed girl time.

I hoped their presence would help me to stop obsessing over Carter. He'd made his choice, and I had to live with it. It didn't matter that I hadn't told him how I felt, or that I was so stupid I'd only asked him what he thought. He was a guy. It was possible that he believed I wasn't interested and blew me off to save face.

But the universe continued to save me from myself. I'd gone back the next day like a crazed stalker. Carter hadn't been there. That had been a blessing in disguise and a sign to let sleeping dogs lie. I hadn't had a clue what I was going to say. And, *"Hey, I realize we don't know each other all that well, but I think I'm falling for you,"* sounded crazy, even to me.

Honestly, neither of us knew the other. Maybe this was the world's way of keeping us from finding out. If I'd had to bet, Carter wouldn't have liked what he would have run into when involved in my world. On the surface, I was an heiress to a vast financial fortune. People assumed that left me vapid and bankrolled. I played into that persona when I went out, but it wasn't who I was. I cared about my job and the people I worked with, and I loved my friends. The fact that I hadn't settled down didn't say anything about my ability to commit just that I hadn't found the person worth committing to. I was young, and I'd never worried about it...until now. Thinking that man had finally made an appearance in my life only for me to let him go felt worse than believing I'd always be alone.

"We should go out for a night on the town." Riley rubbed my back and gave me a sympathetic glance. "It'll help you take your mind off things."

I sighed and rolled over on the bed and faced my two best friends. We'd spent the day stuffing our faces with room service...and wine. Thankfully, Gabby hadn't had to work, so they were both here trying to keep me from wallowing in depression.

But I fought their efforts at every turn. "I don't know. I don't feel like going anywhere for a while." I pouted. I'd only experienced one break-up—not that this could be classified as one—and sadly, this was more devastating than the fact that my house had gone up in flames and I'd lost everything I owned in one fell swoop.

Gabby laughed and patted my leg. "As long as you aren't setting any more fires for entertainment."

I swatted at her hand. "It was an accident." A loud humph came from my mouth unexpectedly. "I feel bad enough that I almost killed my poor neighbors and left countless people home-less without your making it worse." I swallowed back the memory and tried to focus on how grateful I was that I hadn't had any lingering side effects—no soreness in my chest or throat—unless I counted my heartache. And my dad had dealt with the insurance company for both the building and my personal belongings, so that was one less thing for me to stress over.

"Well, you didn't cost anyone their life. And, an insanely hot firefighter carried you in the safety of his arms away from the danger." Riley was overly animated, and while I wanted to smack her for romanticizing the situation with Carter, I couldn't stop myself from laughing at the wistful gleam in her eyes and dopey grin on her face.

Gabby stayed focused on the problem at hand instead of the fictional world Riley currently resided in. "You should try to talk to him, Brayleigh. At the very least, tell him how you feel so you'll know beyond a shadow of a doubt that it wouldn't work out. Otherwise, you'll always wonder if he was just protecting himself, thinking he'd never be in your league." Her voice of reason had always been reliable, but that sounded batshit crazy. She'd apparently missed the detail about a one-night stand —there was never supposed to be a repeat.

It was just supposed to have been fun. I had no clue how I ended up in that situation. I chuckled to myself in a less than genuine laugh —falling asleep with a lit candle and knocking it over was *how* I'd ended up here. The real question was, why was Carter the one to respond to the call? I wanted to let him go, but Gabby was right; I'd never be able to do so until I knew for certain I'd exhausted all avenues, and that meant getting out my feelings.

"Okay."

They stayed with me until Gabby had to go to work and Riley opted for a hookup, or a date, or whatever—I'd stopped paying attention to her explanation once I'd realized it involved a man. Riley had offered to stick it out at the hotel, but there was no reason for both of us to be miserable. And once they'd left, I tried like hell to convince myself to stop feeling bad about something I couldn't control.

Even if I wanted to give Carter one last shot, I didn't have a number to reach him, and there was no way I was going to his house again after I'd mailed his clothes back to him. After hours at war with my mind, I resolved myself to one truth. I had tried with Carter, and I wouldn't be trying again. A clean break was better, and I'd get over it faster.

After a hot shower, I snuggled up in some of the cute pajamas Riley had lent me—I still hadn't bothered to go shopping—and moved to the living room area of the hotel suite to watch television. I found myself lost in a baking show, debating on the icing choices of the contestants. I'd hit an all-time low if this was better than fixating on Carter's not caring about me the way I did him. I was failing at life.

As much as I didn't want to know that he was at work, I did. I'd kept up with his schedule and the rotation. Twenty-four on, forty-eight off. If I were going to contact him, the station would be the only way to do it. It was a stretch. The likelihood that he'd be there and not out on a call was slim, but I couldn't stop myself.

I got myself together, searched for the phone number to the firehouse, and took a deep, cleansing breath. As I waited for it to ring, a knot formed in my throat, nearly strangling me.

"District Fire Department, how can I help you?" A chipper male answered the line, and I wondered if he was a dispatcher or firefighter.

"May I speak to Carter?" I trailed off, realizing I didn't even know his last name.

"He's not in right now. He ran out of here like a cat with its ass on fire—something about his girlfriend. Hell, I don't know. I can't keep up with these guys. Can I take a message?"

That knot that had formed in my throat not only kept me from breathing, it kept me from answering. I just hung up and dropped the phone into my lap. I'd heard him correctly; he said girlfriend. And that meant that Carter had played me.

All the pieces started to fall into place, and the puzzle made more sense once the picture came together. He had told me nothing about himself the night we'd met. Carter had intended it to be a one-night stand just like I had but for different reasons. They might not live together—since there were no female items in his house—but Carter had been honest when he said I was nothing more than sex. And it certainly justified why he'd been so desperate for me to leave so quickly, without any warning.

Carter had a girlfriend. I really was *just* sex.

I felt stupid, but more than that, I felt used.

Collapsing on the bed, I cried myself to sleep, hoping that tomorrow would be a better day.

Chapter Ten

CARTER

I was zoned out in the rec room at the station...thinking.

Last night, I'd rushed into a house and brought someone out to safety. When I'd handed the woman over to the EMTs, I'd hoped she was all right, but there wasn't some inner pull to check on her. She had been left in capable hands, and that was it. I'd done my job, and it had been time to let the paramedics do theirs. I hadn't asked her to hang out at my house. I hadn't told her where my spare key was. I certainly hadn't raced home in hopes of seeing her. Hell, I hadn't really even wondered what she'd do after the engine pulled away.

It was Brayleigh—not the incident—that

warranted that reaction and garnered that response. And it wasn't just the fact that she was drop-dead gorgeous and completely out of my league. It was *her*. She'd casually asked about my day, and something as simple as that made her stand out. It was the first time in ages that anyone had cared how my shift went that didn't already know.

And for the first time, I'd believed I was worth that. Maybe I'd found a woman who thought loving me for a day or a year was worth the possibility of losing me in a fire tomorrow or a decade from now. That was more important than ensuring no one ever cared about me, so they never had to face my loss.

It was entirely possible things might go really badly with Brayleigh, but the notion that they might be blissfully right so far outweighed the negative. It took a special woman to love a firefighter, and if I'd found her, there was no way in hell I could let her go.

"Dude, are you asleep?" Nick slapped my leg, sitting next to me on the sofa.

I'd been dodging Nick and Brian both. They'd nagged the hell out of me since the day Brayleigh had left, and I couldn't stand hearing constant reminders of how I'd fucked up. I also hadn't wanted to admit they were right.

But they were.

"No. Just thinking." I popped open my eyes and yawned. It had been a long night, and I was ready for it to be over.

"About your screw up?" Nick cackled, and I gave him a side eye.

I frowned and shook my head. "No, just...I don't know." I thought about it for a split second and decided I was burning daylight—even though it was dark—and I needed to act. I kicked the footrest of the reclining sofa back in and hopped up. "I'm going to run an errand. Tell Captain I'm sick or something." I waved my hand to dismiss him.

Nick stared at me from the couch dumbstruck. Firefighters didn't just abandon their shift. "Where the fuck are you going?" He chuckled.

I grinned. "To get my girl."

THANK GOD BRAYLEIGH'D HAD THE mindset to mail my shit back to me; otherwise, I wouldn't have had a clue where to find her. I'd driven by her building several times, and it was months away from being inhabitable.

Feeling out of place in my jeans and hoodie, I walked through the swank lobby of a hotel I'd never be able to afford. It was clearly for the privileged, and as a firefighter, that was something I'd never be. This wasn't the type of place State Farm housed their average customer based on a run-of-the-mill policy. Either Brayleigh had some elite insurance membership, or there'd been an upgrade involved. Hell, I didn't even know what the girl did for a living. There was so much I didn't know, which had been my argument against the pull I had toward her. You couldn't love someone you didn't know. It wasn't possible. Despite that belief, here I was prepared to make a proclamation that dispelled that theory.

I sauntered up to the front desk with far more confidence than I actually felt and waited for someone to help me. I dinged the bell, and an older gentleman came from the back. When he lifted his head, I recognized him as the father of one of the guys at the station.

"Hey, Mr. Roper." I smiled and shook his

hand over the counter. "I had no idea you worked here."

"Carter, what brought you in?" His brow furrowed, and his weathered skin wrinkled with worry. "Is there something on fire I didn't know about? Damn kids around here." Mr. Roper glanced to both sides and then leaned over the counter. "Spoiled brats, the lot of them. Parents don't watch a single thing these kids do and then sue the hotel when they get hurt." He righted himself, shaking his head in disgust.

Grumpy old men made me laugh. I had no idea what Mr. Roper was doing working in a customer service position since he didn't really seem to care for people. "No, sir." I couldn't stop the chuckle that rolled through me as he glared at two teenage boys who'd just left trash on a lobby table. "Maybe you can help me."

He waved at the litter and spoke loudly enough for the boys to hear. "Of course, I'm here to serve. Apparently, my duties hosting the front desk now also include trash pickup."

One of the kids gave Mr. Roper the middle finger right before he stepped onto the elevator. There was no way in hell I could work with these kinds of people. He finally returned his attention to me and raised his brow.

"I'm looking for someone." I put my hands on the marble counter, leaned in, and lowered my voice. "I'm hoping you can tell me what room she's in."

Mr. Roper started to shake his head before I'd even finished asking the question. "Son, I like you, but you know I can't do that. I can't give out a guest's information."

I closed my eyes, ran my hand through my hair, and sighed. When I looked at him again, sympathy marred his previously irritated expression. "I know, but, it's important." I hadn't thought this through. I had no idea Mr. Roper worked here, and if I couldn't get *him* to give me her room number, I'd be dead in the water with a stranger. "She's an incredible girl that I—well, I screwed things up with."

He stared at me as if dumbfounded that I believed those few words would convince him to risk losing his job.

"Would it help if I told you she might be dying?" I was desperate and grasping at straws.

His eyes went wide. "Is she?"

I shrugged. "I mean, she could be. I pulled

her out of a fire a few days ago, so it's possible." I laughed at the stupidity of this conversation.

Mr. Roper's shoulders sank with his heavy sigh. "So we're going with a medical emergency, and you were the nearest emergency responder in the neighborhood?"

If that's how he needed to spin things, I wouldn't argue.

"Youth these days. All think the world and the law should bend to their whims," he muttered under his breath while I held mine. "What's her name?"

"Brayleigh."

He arched his brow as if to ask for more, and I sensed the sheepish expression that crossed my face. I felt like an idiot when I couldn't give him her last name. It had been on the damn box, but for the life of me, I couldn't think of it.

"Luckily for you, it's not a common name. She's in the penthouse." He clicked away on the keyboard, reached under the counter and produced a card, and stuck it in the machine. "You'll need a key to access that floor." Mr. Roper held it out, but when I went to take it, he snatched it back. "Don't go using this card to force your way in there, son. She turns you away at the door, you take it like a man. Understand?"

"Fully."

I took the card and dashed toward the elevators the two jackasses who'd ticked off Mr. Roper had taken. My heart pounded the way it did during a fire, and my breathing became just as labored. I'd never felt the adrenaline rush that came from entering a burning building in any other facet of life. Yet here I stood, thinking I had seconds to get to her before I lost her for good.

When I pushed the *P* for the top floor, I had to insert my card, and I briefly wondered what the hell she was doing here...all the way up there. My chest constricted, and my ribs ached with each ding of the elevator as I rose. At this rate, I'd pass out or hyperventilate before I even knocked on the door.

But when the moment came, I was still conscious, and the thud of my fist on the wood echoed in my mind like the chiming of bells, low and hollow.

The door swung open, and time stopped.

I'd forgotten just how damned beautiful

she was. Her curly hair was tossed into a messy bun on top of her head, and little wisps swept across her forehead and framed her face. I took her in from top to toe, including her cute pajamas that hid her stunning figure. In that moment, I didn't give a shit about her body. Her eyes were rimmed red and puffy from crying, her nose was pink, and sadness clung to her expression.

The tightness in my chest almost suffocated me, knowing I could be responsible for that. I wanted nothing more than to reach out and pull her into my arms to ease both of our discomfort, but I couldn't force that. Not yet.

Her eyes went wide, and her lips parted in shock. "Carter?"

I cleared my throat, but every time I tried to find words, my mouth went dry, and my vocal cords refused to function. "Hey, Brayleigh." I stuffed my hands into my pocket so she wouldn't see me trying to wipe the sweat off my palms.

"What are you doing here?" The confidence she'd shown in every interaction we'd had was nowhere to be found. Her voice was weak, and she appeared exhausted.

I couldn't hack through the tension with an ax, but it was time to man up and take it on the chin if that's what Brayleigh chose to dish out. "I was hoping we could talk." Those words should never come from a man's mouth.

Her hesitation was palpable and also a proverbial kick to the gut. I swallowed hard, and my mouth went dry. Acrid.

Brayleigh moved back, taking the door with her. It was a silent invitation to come inside, but I took it with a sigh of relief. One hurdle crossed; God only knew how many more I had to go.

Despite how plush and extravagant the room was when I stepped inside, its opulence did nothing to deter the feeling that I'd sent her here...to suffer. I'd made her a castaway. She was Tom Hanks, and this was her island. It was ludicrous, but that didn't stop me from shouldering the blame.

She allowed the door to close behind me, although she didn't follow me farther inside. Her arms were folded across her chest, and despite how tired she appeared, her expression was hard. That wall she'd built when I last saw her stood solid and strong. This wasn't going to be as easy as just apologizing. I'd told her I used her for sex, and regardless of whether that had been how she'd started things with me, no woman wanted to feel unworthy of more.

"I'm sorry, Brayleigh." I dug my hands deeper into my pockets while her face remained unchanged. "I'm not very good at this—"

Brayleigh pursed her pouty lips and arched a sculpted brow. "At what? Lying?"

"Wait. What?" I hadn't been truthful about my feelings for her, but I wouldn't have called it lying. That implied malicious intent, and whether she wanted to believe it or not, I'd done it to protect her, not me.

"Why are you here?" She and I hadn't done tons of talking, but I'd yet to hear the snide way she'd just lashed out.

This was going to be harder than I'd antici-pated; so much for my charm and good looks getting me anywhere with Brayleigh. "To apologize."

She dropped her arms to her side, and I couldn't help but notice the way she balled her hands into fists that trembled as she spoke. "I know you have a girlfriend. Does she know you're here?"

I stared at her in shock. She'd seemed fine after the fire, but now I wondered if she had lingering damage from smoke inhalation. My lips parted, closed, parted again—nothing came out. I didn't have a damn clue what Brayleigh was talking about, but trying to dispel that myth would be difficult if I didn't speak.

"Did you think I wouldn't find out?" She huffed an agitated breath. "You must think I'm stupid. Newsflash, I'm not. I'm just prone to picking the wrong men."

I laughed once without humor and nearly choked on what I was about to say. "I don't have a girlfriend." My tongue swept across my chapped lips. "That's the whole reason we're in this mess."

Brayleigh's anger softened into confusion. "What does that mean?"

"It means that you're mistaken. I don't have a girlfriend." It was painful to admit that while I had game, it ended when we put on our clothes. "I have trouble with that sort of thing— relationships I mean." I took a deep breath and prepared myself to admit my greatest flaw. "That's why I let you leave so fast."

"You're going to have to do better than that because nothing you're saying makes the least bit of sense."

"I was afraid I'd get attached to you. Or that you would to me. I panicked, so when you gave me an out, I took it." I dared to reach out for her hand, but she pulled back. "Brayleigh, I was wrong. That's why I'm here." It might not change anything, but just to have expelled that truth felt like that first breath of fresh air after I took off my helmet.

"Carter..." Her tone indicated she wasn't buying what I tried to sell.

Brayleigh finally left the door and headed into the enormous suite. This damn place was bigger than my house. She sat on the edge of a leather couch that probably cost what I made in six months. I stepped forward with hesitation, but she didn't shut me down.

"I realize that it doesn't make a lot of sense to you. Hell, since I've spent the last few days analyzing it, it doesn't make a whole lot to me anymore. But I swear, if you give me the chance to explain, you'll know I'm sincere." I took a seat at her side, not too close as to invade her space, but not so far that I couldn't reach her when she finally gave me the green light. "What made you think I have a girlfriend?"

Her gaze fell to the floor with what appeared to be shame. "I called the fire station earlier to try to find you." She picked at her cuticles in her lap. "The guy who answered said you were out with your girlfriend." When she lifted her eyes, they welled with tears. She was adorably innocent but distraught.

I wanted to laugh, like a hearty chuckle from deep in my belly. I'd bet I had Nick to blame for this shit. "It was probably one of my friends, and he was likely talking about you."

"Why would he be talking about me?" She blanched and got defensive.

I gave up fighting the urge. She was within reach, and I needed to touch her, to feel her skin on mine. I was desperate to inhale her sweet scent and kiss her soft lips. I had to be cautious, but I didn't think she'd push me away.

Her skin was warm under my fingers, and she leaned her jaw into my touch.

"Because I said I was going to get my girl."

Chapter Eleven

My stomach flipped around itself as I sank farther into the cushions. I wanted to smile—in fact, I probably was—but I was so unaware of my body that I couldn't be sure.

Carter smirked at whatever expression graced my face. "I want you, Brayleigh. I don't know why it happened or how, I just— I don't want to be without you. Not anymore."

I let out a heavy sigh, blinking back confusion. He'd summed up my feelings, but regardless, I couldn't jump into something that I couldn't get out of. Carter had already done a number on my emotional state, and at some point, I had to resume life as an adult and leave this hotel.

"Why now?" I asked.

Carter dropped his hand and tilted his head, confusion now laying heavy on his brow. "What?"

I sat up straight and tried to pull myself together instead of allowing myself to become putty in his fully capable palm. "You said you don't do relationships. Why now? What makes me different?" An uneasy laugh parted my lips. "I don't want to be the woman who starts out trying to change you. That would never work, and you'd end up resenting me, Carter."

"I'm already changed, Brayleigh. No—changed isn't even the right word. It was—" He stumbled over his thoughts as his mouth tried unsuccessfully to catch up with his brain. "Look." He shifted from the couch next to me to a spot on the coffee table in front of me.

The warmth of Carter's hands on my knees nearly had me throwing caution to the wind and telling him we'd figure things out under the sheets. "When I graduated from the academy, one of the guys I'd been enrolled with died in a fire we both fought. At his funeral, I saw his wife—God, she was so young with a baby on her hip. His baby—mourning the love of her life. My heart ached for her, and I didn't even know her."

"But that wasn't your fault?" It came off as a question, but I already knew the answer.

Carter was still visibly affected by the event. "It didn't matter. The only thing that mattered was that I never left a woman standing next to a grave with my baby in her arms or my child at her side. If I never let myself love anyone, then they could never love me. No strings, no damage."

My head bobbed slowly as understanding crossed my mind. "And you think if you're never in a relationship that no one will ever love you. And if no one ever loves you, then you would never be leaving anyone behind..." I could hardly breathe just thinking about what kind of commitment that kind of loyalty to a profession took not to mention the toll on the man who'd made it.

"I'm not going to lie to you again, Brayleigh." He took a deep breath and held my stare. "I absolutely have feelings for you. I haven't stopped thinking about you since the night we met at Right Nine. And the thought of what that could mean for you down the road scares the shit out of me. But not having the chance to share a future with you scares me more." Carter pulled his lips between his teeth and waited.

Losing him to a fire had never crossed my mind since I'd never really had him. I couldn't fathom the pain of becoming a widow, but I knew it would be worth any amount of time that I had gotten to spend loving Carter.

"I want to be with you, too, Carter," I whispered, unsure of what that meant to a man like him.

The smile that lifted the corners of his mouth and widened his eyes confirmed that whatever it meant, Carter was in. "Really?"

I giggled. "Yes."

In a flash, Carter had come off the table, sinking both of us into the couch as he laid over me. His plump lips met mine, and he coaxed my mouth open with the slip of his tongue. I didn't resist or restrain myself when I allowed him to settle between my thighs. God, I'd missed his touch, the feel of his weight on me, his arms, his abs—just *him*. My hands searched for bare skin while his kiss sought to turn me on. The velvety feel of his taut biceps gave way to firm forearms, and just as I found the hem of his T-shirt, he ground his erection against me.

I clawed at his shirt when he sat up, breaking the kiss only to remove clothing. And in a panic, he stripped me of what I had on. I hadn't seen where any of our clothing went, and I didn't care. It could be hanging off the balcony as long as I got Carter. He chuckled before crushing his lips to mine.

"Carter, touch me. *Please.*" I moaned against his mouth. And by touch, I meant take.

He smirked as he pulled away, kissing the edge of my lips. Carter worked his way down the curves of my body until he slipped his fingers between my folds. I was wet and ready and totally unashamed of what he did to me. The circle of his thumb on my clit sent my spine into an arch McDonald's would be proud of, and then he dipped two thick fingers inside.

My cry of pleasure filled the room, and when he curled his fingers into my G-spot that moan became a scream. "Oh, God." I could barely breathe between the waves of euphoria, and I was afraid to gasp for breath for fear of missing one. I swirled around the edge of orgasm, desperate for Carter to take me to the place only he could.

But he held back with a satisfied grin. I narrowed my eyes when I realized the game he played, the way he tried to taunt me into his web. I was already so tangled up in him there was no way to trap me further, but if he wanted to drag this out, I'd be happy to oblige. He shifted, and I took the opportunity to wrap my hands around his thick cock.

"Mmm, careful, babe." He closed his eyes as I stroked, but that didn't stop his ministrations between my legs. "This will be over before you want it to be."

I didn't bother to respond with words; instead, I spread my legs wide, exposing my swollen, wet pussy and hoped he'd take the invitation. I didn't care how quickly it was over. I'd waited days to see him, to have him touch me. We could fuck all night if that's what it came down to; we'd done it before, and I wasn't above doing it again.

His lids parted when my legs moved. Carter's clear-blue eyes went wide, and his pupils surged. The moment his nostrils flared, he'd lost control. He sat back on his haunches, pulling himself free from my grasp.

I didn't catch what he'd muttered under his breath. "What?" I had no clue what had sent him from heated passion to pissed off in a hair's breadth.

"No condom." He tugged on the roots of his hair, clearly unhappy.

I shouldn't be flippant about safe sex, but I hadn't been with anyone unprotected, and I was on the pill. Based on Carter's reaction, he didn't make a habit of tapping without wrapping. So, I threw caution to the wind and hoped it didn't bite me in the ass later. "I've been on birth control for a long time. So, unless you rebounded—"

"Fuck no. I haven't been with anyone else."

I shrugged and raised my eyebrows, still waiting for him to take the invitation before I jumped him and forced it upon him.

Carter smirked, and I lost a piece of me in that smile. "You think I'd turn down an opportunity to go bareback with you?"

There wasn't a chance to respond to that rhetorical question before he thrusted into me, stealing my breath and ability to speak. The initial plunge was hard and deep, but when I'd expected him to fuck, he shifted gears. His hips rolled at a slower pace, still as forceful just not pounding. I wasn't sure that Carter could make love, but he certainly fucked me like he cared about me. There was a huge difference. He managed to be rough yet thorough. It was the shift in his eyes; the gleam had softened. Even though Carter tossed me around, giving me what he wanted me to have, he did so with me in mind.

My nails raked down his back, sliding over his taut ass that clenched as he drove into me. "Don't stop, Carter." I was so close, and this was damn near perfect.

He slid his forearm under the small of my back and lifted me into his lap. "Wasn't planning on it, babe." Carter's warm lips met mine as he encouraged me to ride his engorged cock.

I climbed higher, clenching around him as I rose to the delicious peak of an orgasm. But Carter didn't make me take the trip alone. With nothing between us, his hot dick speared into me as he thrusted up and my hips slammed down. He drove deep and stilled, spilling his come into me while I came around him. I collapsed against his sweaty skin, draping my arms around his nape and tucking my face into his neck.

He moaned and twitched but never let me go. "You're amazing, Brayleigh." His murmured words were warm against my ear and settled into my heart.

He didn't rush me out of his lap or try to move. Carter merely shifted us on the couch, with his back to the cushions so he could relax. There he trailed his fingers down my spine and circled patterns on my skin. And every once in a while, he'd kiss my temple or drop his lips to my bare shoulder. The longer we were there, the harder it was to imagine anything better than this.

Carter moved my hair that had fallen from the knot on top of my head, tucking it behind my ear. "You hungry, babe?" His tone was deeper, softer, more tender.

I shifted in his arms but not out of them. If I could have stayed right where I was forever, I would never move. "I could eat." My stomach gurgled like someone had asked for its opinion. "But I can't do any more hotel food. I'm sick of it." I grimaced, hating that I'd just admitted I'd been holed up here for as many days as he and I had been apart.

"We can go back to my place."

I wanted to believe that an apology and sex could fix things, but I was skeptical. "For how long?" Whether I liked it or not, I was still in an awkward position between insurance companies, hotel rooms, and apartments.

"For however long you want to stay." Carter shrugged like he hadn't just insinuated that I come for an extended amount of time.

I pulled back in his lap but didn't leave the security of his arms. "What?" I had to have misunderstood.

His crystal-blue eyes went steely grey, and his expression turned serious. "I meant what I said, Brayleigh. I don't want to be away from you." He swallowed, kissed my lips, and sat back. "I have to go to work, but that doesn't mean I can't come home to you. I'm all in."

I wasn't prone to spontaneity, but I also wasn't inclined to fall in love. Carter brought out the desire to do both, and I was in a position to take him up on the offer with little fanfare. I didn't have any furniture or stuff; hell, I didn't even have any of my own clothes. "Okay." I pressed my lips to his, and he smiled against my kiss.

"Yeah?" he asked.

I nodded with a smile.

Carter cradled my face in his large hands and gave me a serious look. "Just don't light any candles."

I was so blissfully fucking happy that I felt like a fraud, one of those dudes on TV that had the perfect life, or at least what seemed like it.

The difference was, I actually had it with Brayleigh.

She'd moved in that night after we left the hotel, and we'd spent the last few months getting to know each other and finding the groove of our life together. It had taken some adjustments when I'd realize *who* she was and the lifestyle she was accustomed to, but that had been my issue, not hers. Not once had Brayleigh ever made me feel like the life we had together was less than the one she'd come from; in fact, she'd made me feel like a god who lavished her with everything she'd ever wanted. And not one bit of it cost a penny.

The closer we got, the more I hated to be away from her. Twenty-four-hour shifts were hard, but coming home to her always made the day before worth it. Brayleigh would always be worth whatever I had to go through to get back to her side. There was a reason I'd had to have her the night I met her at her dad's club; I just hadn't known then that it was destiny, divine intervention. Brayleigh made me a better man, plain and simple.

"Are you sure you want to do this?" Nick gave me a funny look.

I smacked him upside the back of the head. "You're supposed to encourage me, jackass, not talk me out of it."

Nick rubbed the back of his head—I hadn't hit him that hard—and grimaced. "I'd be a shit friend if I didn't make certain this was the right thing to do."

"Dude, seriously, I'm sure."

He clapped me on the shoulder and shook

his head. "Another one bites the dust. Next thing I know you're going to want babies. What's this world coming to?"

Nick could goad me all he wanted, but he was just as happy for Brayleigh and me as Brian and Erika were. Nick wasn't anywhere near ready to settle down, but he'd welcomed Brayleigh into our fold, and we'd all do the same whenever he found his forever.

By the time I'd left the station, nothing could have dissuaded me. It probably wasn't the romantic gesture she deserved, but if she wanted a man who made public ordeals out of private moments, I wasn't that guy. Thankfully, she wasn't that girl. At least not anymore. Once the paparazzi had figured out she'd settled down, and her father gave up on getting her back to New York, our lives were fairly low-key.

She was on the couch, working with the TV on when I came through the door. Brayleigh did her best to keep the same schedule I did. It enabled her to keep the scanner on so she knew where I was and what calls I'd answered, and she could spend as much time with me when I was at the house if we did the same things at the same times. It was unconventional. I didn't know another fireman whose girl doted on him the way mine did me, and it was just one more box I ticked off on the list of reasons I needed to make this legal.

The moment I saw her, my plans shifted. She had her hair up in a bun, wearing one of my shirts with her legs exposed—there was a fifty-fifty chance of her having on panties underneath—and I was instantly aroused at the sight of so much of her skin.

"You're home." Brayleigh tossed her laptop aside and hopped up from the couch. Every morning, I got the same welcome. Without fail, she jumped into my arms, wrapping her arms around my neck and legs around my waist. Her excitement was contagious, and I was the luckiest fucking man in the world.

I laughed. "Hey, babe." I kissed her, tasted her, memorized the way she held me. Every morning after a shift, I thanked God for getting me safely through each call and back to her. And every morning, I kissed her like it was the first time.

She moaned against me, sliding her fingers

into my hair. I was starving and tired, but I wanted Brayleigh's attention more—I always wanted her more. More than anything. With her wrapped around me like a finger monkey, I walked us to our bedroom.

I laid her on the bed, stripped, and got on after her. The greatest thing about sex in a committed relationship was the ability to be uninhibited. There were times we took things slow, others were quick, some were hard, or soft, but regardless, it never mattered because it was always with Brayleigh.

She laughed, took off her shirt—no panties—and spread her thighs to welcome my hips. Her body felt like coming home after a shift. It was safe, loving, secure...perfect. The dip of her sides and the swell of her breasts, they teased my senses and never failed to arouse me. I loved Brayleigh's body, but I loved her heart more. And that was the difference I'd never been able to pinpoint when this had started between the two of us. Her heart spoke a language mine understood. There would never be anyone else.

I slid into her warmth and kissed her lips. "Marry me."

Her swollen lips parted, and her beautiful

brown irises shimmered. "What?" She laughed, but it was uncertainty, not humor.

"I love you. I want you to be my wife." I didn't do eloquent, and I couldn't get any simpler than that.

She held my face in her hands, and her eyes began to water. When her lip trembled, I nearly came undone. "Okay."

"Yeah?"

"Yes." Brayleigh managed to nod as she shouted out the words I desperately wanted to hear. "I'll marry—"

I kissed her hard before she could finish, and I lifted her onto my lap as she squealed. There, I held my fiancé and slipped into her again. Brayleigh clutched me as I rocked her, squeezing her ass and guiding her movement as she went.

"You feel so damned good, baby." I tucked my head into the crook of her neck as I rolled with her.

"You do, too. Always." Her nails scratched at my scalp, and she tugged on my hair the deeper I went.

The only thing better than the way she

clawed at my skin when I fucked her was the added heat that surrounded me when she got close to the edge. Her insides would tense and release and squeeze my cock in a choke hold I never wanted to end. Brayleigh had taken over the rhythm in my lap which freed up a hand to tease her clit. I slid my thumb over her sensitive nub and brought her right up to the edge with me.

She cried out, one of her beautiful orgasms took over, and she collapsed in my arms. I held her tightly as I emptied myself into her.

"I love you, Carter." Her whispered words fell against my neck, and I kissed her temple, refusing to let her go.

"I love you, too, Brayleigh. More than you'll ever know."

Brayleigh

"You look beautiful." Riley situated my veil around my shoulders and down my back for about the hundredth time. Her eyes glistened with unshed tears of happiness when she stared at me through the mirror. "Carter's a lucky man, Bray."

"Thank you." I was a lucky girl, too.

I stared in the mirror at the understated gown I'd chosen and thought about how different my life had turned out in comparison to what I'd thought it would as a child. My parents had pushed for an over-the-top, New York socialite-style wedding, but I'd insisted on small and intimate. The press would have a field day no matter what I did, so I made sure the day was for Carter and me.

In a few minutes, my dad would walk me down the aisle to meet the guy who waited for me at the altar. I couldn't have designed a better man or relationship and wondered how I'd ever gotten so lucky as to knock over a candle and burn down an entire building.

Riley wiped her tears of happiness away and changed the conversation before she ruined her makeup. "Gabby is ordering around the caterers. Apparently, they keep getting things wrong." She fluffed the bottom of my dress and grabbed my hand with a squeeze.

I turned from the mirror to face my best friend and smiled. "Figures."

"You nervous?"

I shook my head, careful not to mess up my hair. "Not even a little. Just ready."

"You and Carter are perfect together." She hugged my neck, careful of my updo.

"I'm back." Gabby barged in, breathless but still smiling. "The shrimp are now in the right place." She needed to feel useful, and I needed to eat—it worked for both of us.

"Are you ready?" Riley asked me.

I nodded. I'd been ready. A part of me had known when I'd first laid eyes on him; I just hadn't recognized it for what it was.

Carter grinned from ear to ear when the church doors opened and I stepped foot into the sanctuary. I'd expected my heart to pound and my hands to sweat, but peace washed over me, and everything about this felt right.

We'd fallen in love so fast that at times I wondered if either of us had ever really stood a chance against the push fate gave us. The way we loved each other was all-consuming, and whether I got him for fifty years or fifty days, I'd thank God for each one.

My dad squeezed my hand when I took his arm and whispered in my ear. "You look beautiful, sweetheart." My father didn't give me the line about still being able to get out of this or his dealing with disappointed guests. He knew Carter was perfect for me, and despite how much he'd wanted me to marry a particular type of man with a specific social status, my dad knew Carter loved me. At the end of the day, that was all my father had cared about—how much my husband cared for me, not how many houses he could buy, or dollars were in his bank account.

When my dad handed me off to Carter, he clapped him on the shoulder. "Love her well, son."

Carter nodded and took my hand. And in that moment, no one else existed. I was the only woman in his world, and he was the only man in mine.

There, at the altar, in front of our closest family and friends, Carter and I vowed to love each other through thick and thin. We made that commitment together, and I couldn't help but think how ironic it was that this had been born from a girl who'd just wanted to have a good time and a guy who'd wanted no strings.

The End

Click or scan the QR code to check out other books by Mila Hart

Acknowledgments

Thank you to all the bloggers who gave Mila Hart a shot when you had so many other options.

And thank you to all the readers who took a chance on a newbie author.

xoxo
mila

It all started with two best friends and a whole lot of dirty ideas…

MILA HART is your go-to for cheeky, steamy, and seriously spicy reads. We're all about quick, hot stories that get your heart racing and leave you wanting more—but here's the twist: we give you both the heat and the story.

With tons of deliciously sexy tales in the works, get ready for the perfect mix of plot and passion—because we're just getting started!

Check us out at:
www.authormilahart.com